Free Marcus Katz!!!

A Curated Collection of Yelp Reviews

A Novel

Free Marcus Katz!!!

A Curated Collection of Yelp Reviews

A Novel

Howard Marc Chesley

ROUNDFIRE
BOOKS

Winchester, UK
Washington, USA

JOHN HUNT PUBLISHING

First published by Roundfire Books, 2022
Roundfire Books is an imprint of John Hunt Publishing Ltd., No. 3 East St., Alresford,
Hampshire SO24 9EE, UK
office@jhpbooks.com
www.johnhuntpublishing.com
www.roundfire-books.com

For distributor details and how to order please visit the 'Ordering' section on our website.

ISBN: 978 1 78904 982 4
978 1 78904 983 1 (ebook)
Library of Congress Control Number: 2021914268

A CIP catalogue record for this book is available from the British Library.

Design: Matthew Greenfield

UK: Printed and bound by CPI Group (UK) Ltd, Croydon, CR0 4YY
Printed in North America by CPI GPS partners

We operate a distinctive and ethical publishing philosophy in
all areas of our business, from our global network of authors to
production and worldwide distribution.

Also by Howard Chesley

Some Books Aren't for Reading, Roundfire Books ISBN 9781785358784

From Marcus Katz

It had never occurred to me that anyone would want to make a book out of Yelp reviews. You can read all of my reviews for free online so I didn't know why anyone would want to pay for them, but out of the blue several months ago an editor, Heather Marsden, at John Hunt Publishing Limited, IM'd me. Heather said she was a "total Yelp junkie" and that she had been following all of my 1400-plus Yelp reviews and she thought if she chose the right ones they could tell a story – my story. Of course I couldn't say no because they were offering money and fame! Anyway, I really hope you like reading my published book and I hope you tell your friends about it.

Barrington Farms Supermarket ★ ★ ★ ★

This is my first review ever for Yelp. I have read many Yelp online reviews in the past but just never had the nerve to post. I do believe if you are a reader of Yelp reviews it is only right to create reviews, just like it is important to vote if you live in a democracy or to put money in the church collection plate after a good sermon, although I really don't go to church because I am Jewish by birth, and I don't go to synagogue either. Anyway, I am sorry for not being more proactive. I am now writing this review of Barrington Farms Market because I hope it will bring needed change. When I spoke to Dr. DeSantis about my plan to post about Barrington Farms on Yelp she agreed that it might be an effective way for me to get the outcome I want and also it would be a safe way for me to "reach out." "Reach out" is a phrase that Dr. DeSantis uses too often in my opinion. I am having some personal issues regarding my mother's current illness and I think that Dr. DeSantis believes I am keeping too much bottled inside. Barrington Farms is more expensive than most of the other markets. It has very high quality food and the lines are shorter than they are at Ralph's and Von's. Some people say the checkout people are more attentive, although I personally like it better if my checker chats with the bagger instead of insisting on asking me how my day is. I don't understand why they would care or why it is even polite. The main reason I shop there is that only Barrington Farms sells my favorite ice cream, Van Leeuwen chocolate, a premium brand made with high quality plantation chocolate. So what is the problem you might ask? The last time I went in to buy ice cream and some other things I needed they were blasting sixties Herb Alpert Tijuana Brass music through speakers in the ceiling. The song was "Brave Bull" and it features a piercing solo trumpet. It's not that I don't enjoy music. In fact I sing tenor in the Santa Monica Congregational Church Concert Choir. It's just that I have a strong sensitivity to the blaring of a trumpet. Some people may find this hard to appreciate, but for me a trumpet sound is painful, like fingernails on a blackboard to other people, and I realized I had to leave with just the Van Leeuwen and a package of Bear Naked granola I had in my basket. When the woman at the register asked if I had "found everything I was looking for" I probably should just have nodded "yes," but instead I told her the truth, that I didn't appreciate the loud trumpet music and had to quit shopping. She said she didn't think it was that loud, but I disagreed and there must have been something in the way I said it that disturbed her because then she called the manager over. I told him politely if they were going to continue to play trumpet music I wouldn't be able to shop there anymore. Aspies have difficulty picking up people's reactions, but I could definitely see him grin. Maybe at first he thought I was just kidding but he stopped his smile. Then he told me that most customers enjoy the music (many of their customers are wealthy boomers who probably grew up with Herb Alpert), and that he was sorry if it bothered me, but music was chosen at corporate level and streamed to the store. Then I did something I wish I hadn't done. I told him that he might be in violation of the Americans With Disabilities Act because approximately one person in 59 has an autism spectrum disorder and playing loud, disturbing music in a supermarket technically could be viewed as failing to accommodate a disabled person and there could be legal consequences for Barrington Farms. I don't like playing the disability card. All of my efforts and that of my parents have been to "normalize" me although it sometimes bothers me to try to appear "neurotypical" when I am not. He said he was sorry it bothered me but he had to consider all of his customers and many of them like the music. Barrington Farms is really a five-star supermarket in many people's estimation, and I suppose you get what you pay for, but a honeycrisp apple costs nearly twice as much there as at Ralph's, so I am downgrading it one star for pricing. And then I am downgrading it two stars for the music. I would say that even if most people like trumpet music, it is the responsibility of a public business to make sure that all of its customers are able to shop in an atmosphere that suits them. I am not giving them a poor rating to punish them, but rather, as Dr. DeSantis says, to *reach out* to them and see if they will reconsider. I see that readers can vote this post as "useful," "funny," or "cool." It would be helpful to me to have people vote this as "useful" so that Barrington Farms might take notice.

Response from Barrington Farms

Dear Mr. Katz

We are very sorry that you had an unsatisfactory experience at the Santa Monica Barrington Farms. If you will please contact me at the store I will be happy to see what we can do to ameliorate the situation. We do care about ALL of our customers. Thank you.

Robert Menendez, manager

Update to my review

First I would like to thank the people who voted my post as "useful." There were six of you, which is perhaps less than I had wished for, but it seemed to be enough to make a difference to Barrington Farms. Also the two who thought it was "cool." To those twelve people who voted it "funny" I will say that even though it wasn't necessarily a compliment, it helped anyway as it showed Barrington Farms that people were reading and paying attention to the post even if it wasn't a total endorsement. When I spoke to Mr. Menendez on the phone he apologized for not listening better to a regular customer and said that although he wasn't empowered to reprogram the music, if I would stop by at the manager's desk when I came in they would be happy to turn it off while I shopped. I asked if that would apply to anyone else who was extremely bothered by the music and he said it would. Thanks to Barrington Farms and I am upgrading you to four stars, still with the one-star deduction for price.

Santa Monica Library ★ ★ ★ ★ ★

This will be my second review on Yelp. Hurray! I am now a total Yelp fanboy. I am writing this review partly because my first review of Barrington Farms Market worked so well for me but also because I don't want people to think that because I was so critical that I am some sort of crank. I love Santa Monica Library and because I will always try to be totally honest in my reviews, I should tell you that I work in the library bookstore three days a week so this review is not entirely unprejudiced. My job works out well as I collect money from SSDI for my disability (I have Asperger's syndrome which is on the autism spectrum) and in order to collect I cannot have a job that pays more than $1000 a month, which is a bit more than I get paid by SML—Santa Monica Library, which has a main library and three branches, and a large used book store in the main branch downtown. When book donations come in I help catalogue and categorize them. The library keeps a list of books they might want for the shelves and I put those that I find in a box for one of the main librarians to review. I review the rest to see which ones might be listed for sale by the library association at amazon. com. Some books that are donated can be very valuable. In a box full of old books two months ago I found a rare, signed, first edition copy of *Wind, Sea and Stars* by Antoine de Saint-Exupéry. You may know him because he wrote *The Little Prince*. Exupéry was a professional pilot and wrote several wonderful books about flying. My favorite is *Night Flight*, about flying night mail in Patagonia. In it a mail delivery pilot in a small plane gets caught over the ocean in a williwaw (a very strong offshore wind that comes from the mountains). Although his plane can go 85 mph, the wind is 100 mph against him and he is actually going backwards over the ocean while flying, trying to get to his airfield before he runs out of gas. I won't tell you what happens in the end, but it is a very exciting story. I have 176 books about aviation in my own library and Exupéry is one of my favorite authors. When I showed the book to my supervisor, Helen, she looked it up online and they listed it to sell for $2000. Later she told the head librarian and everyone on the staff about my find and everyone high-fived me. Anyway, I like the Santa Monica Library because it is well run and they have a large number of books for a town library. Although not everyone is rich, Santa Monica is a pretty rich town so I guess they can afford it. Last year they had 1,257,333 checkouts and a population of 92,136 which means that on average every person checks out 13.6 books a year, a very good average for any town. Also they have many computers for people to use. Often, homeless people will use them. Santa Monica has a lot of homeless people because it is sunny and warm and the city offers very good social services. Some of the people are unpleasant and talk out loud or smell, but many of them are quiet and nice. The head librarian tells the staff that we must be polite to all people as much as possible. Perhaps because I have some smaller issues of my own (I know I am very lucky that I have a very nice home—an apartment over my parents' garage) and sometimes people are unkind to me, I feel it is good that the homeless have a place like the library to feel safe. While one of the primary symptoms of Asperger's is an apparent lack of empathy, which is feeling another person's feelings, it doesn't mean that I am incapable of understanding another person's feelings. It's just that I don't get it by some kind of osmosis like neurotypical people do. I have to come to it from a different process from a different part of my brain and the route is not as direct or instant. The library offers speaker programs and movies in their auditorium and if you are researching a particular topic, the reference desk is helpful. If you have a really serious research question, I suggest you try to find Jeanine who works research from 11 a.m. to 6 p.m. Monday through Thursday. She knows how to find almost anything and incidentally she knows quite a bit about the history of Douglas Aircraft as her father used to work for Douglas, which was once located in Santa Monica and we have had some good conversations about that. So if you need to borrow a book, or watch a movie online, or hear a speaker talk about their new book, or buy a good used book from their book store (it is located right outside the parking lot entrance, next to the snack bar), I recommend you try the main branch of Santa Monica Library.

Cedars-Sinai Hospital Cafeteria ★ ★ ★

I have been spending a lot of time for the past few weeks at Cedars-Sinai Hospital. That is because my mother has been sick for some time and it got to a point where her doctors said she needed to be in the hospital to build her strength. I don't want to talk too much about medical issues as it makes me too upset even to think about it. Also I am constantly going back and forth between admiring her doctors and being angry at them, so I don't feel like I can fairly review any doctors or the hospital itself right now. I have eaten many times in the cafeteria here and I think talking about that is a useful distraction for me. I have a lot of spare time to write while Mother is sleeping so this is a great opportunity to write Yelp reviews. The good news about the cafeteria is that the prices are very reasonable and, probably because they are in the business of health, they make an effort to set out healthy food. They have a salad bar and fruit and yogurt. There is a counter where you can order a cold sandwich and a different counter where you can order hot food. Unfortunately, if you order a turkey sandwich they give you slices from a pressed turkey roll and not fresh turkey off the bone. If you want real sliced turkey you should probably go to a good Jewish deli, like Izzie's. Tuna salad is probably a better choice here. If you ask for tomato, it is dry and tasteless. Most people and many restaurants refrigerate tomatoes which is a mistake because sitting in the cold takes away the flavor. The same is true of basil leaves. I haven't actually eaten a hamburger here, but it is also probably a better choice than the turkey sandwich. There is a pretty good chocolate chip cookie that they sell by the cash register and I brought one to my mother in her room and she was able to eat some of it. I think nobody expects to have really good food at a hospital cafeteria and you could say that in this way Cedars-Sinai doesn't disappoint.

Tacos Baja Ensenada ★★★★★

Baja is no humbug!! (I'm trying to get your attention on my restaurant reviews with a catchy opening catch phrase, Yelpers. Is it working?) First, I would like to announce that I have gotten three "useful" votes already for my review of Cedars-Sinai cafeteria and seven "funny" votes. I think this is very good for a new reviewer. I realized that my first review of an eating establishment wasn't very positive. Now I would like to review one of my favorite places so you can all go there. Also I find that I really enjoy writing Yelp reviews so get ready for a bunch more! Like many people in Los Angeles, even those who aren't from Mexico, fish tacos are my very favorite food and there are none better than at Tacos Baja Ensenada on Whittier Boulevard in East Los Angeles. It is fifteen long miles from my home in Santa Monica, but it is always worth the trip. Anyway I enjoy driving in my car. Traveling around in "Atomic Betty," my 1984 Mercedes 300D diesel that was once my grandmother's car in Chicago, is like being in a safe and friendly steel and glass bubble while I look out and enjoy the sights of the city around me. If you are wondering, I am a very good and careful driver and have never been in an accident, but I do stay off the freeways because going that fast near so many cars and trucks makes me nervous, especially because my dad died in a car accident. I first learned of Tacos Baja Ensenada from a Jonathan Gold review. He wrote about food in the *Los Angeles Times* for many years until he died in 2018. He was the first restaurant critic ever to win a Pulitzer Prize for journalism. Mr. Gold wrote "Entire religions have been founded on miracles less profound than the fish taco." Like a lot of dishes people call "street food," a great Baja-style fish taco is a perfect combination of taste and texture. It is made with a piece of fresh, mild white fish, breaded and deep fried, placed inside a warm tortilla and covered with shredded cabbage, cilantro, a mild sauce made with Mexican crema and a dollop of pico de gallo with a slice of lime on the side. All of these are good ingredients, but together they are magic. Tacos Baja Ensenada sells them very reasonably at $2.25 each. Three make a perfect meal. It is a small stand and not very fancy, but there is usually a line at the order window. I must say I am really enjoying sharing this favorite place with you, whoever you are. If you like my review, please vote it as "cool." I think when I have time I will review some of my other favorite fish taco places. You definitely haven't heard the last from me. And then maybe on to pizza (another favorite of mine)!

Palisades Mortuary ★ ★ ★ ★ ★

Palisades Mortuary was really helpful to my family during a very difficult time. When Mother died it seemed like nobody in my family knew what to do. My stepfather, Carl, was very, very sad and found it hard to deal with any of the details. I found him crying alone once. My sister, Lisa, is older than me and the most sensible person in the family. I have never seen Lisa cry. Lisa is a lawyer and she chose Palisades Mortuary because someone in her law firm recommended it. Nobody in the family was in a mood to have to handle all the details and the people at the mortuary promised to take care of everything. I know that when some people get older they like to arrange for their own funerals and burials, but Mother wasn't like that. After the doctors found out that she had stage four pancreatic cancer Lisa tried to talk to her about making arrangements, but Mother said that she was waiting to get into some sort of new clinical drug trial at UCLA hospital and just didn't want to talk about dying. That was fine with me, because I didn't want to talk about dying either. It was really hard on both of us but I think it was harder on her because she was worried about what might happen to me if she was gone. I think it will be difficult for me, but that I will be all right. Anyway, the only thing Lisa and I knew for sure was that Mother wanted to be cremated and have her ashes scattered in the ocean and she didn't want a big funeral, just the family and a few friends. My father, who died seven years ago when his car was hit by a truck on the Foothill Freeway and burned, was already part cremated when they found him, but some other mortuary finished the job. I don't know what happened to his ashes, but since he and my mother were divorced when he died I think they may be in his parents' home in Carmel Valley, California, maybe in an urn on a bookshelf. I know it's weird to think of your dad on a bookshelf, but life is like that. Stephanie at the Palisades Mortuary did tasks like chase after the doctor who forgot to sign the death certificate and went on vacation to Thailand. Also there were documents that I had to sign. Stephanie had to have very good interpersonal skills because Carl and Lisa don't get along that well and Lisa wanted to hire the Neptune Society to scatter Mother's ashes but Carl was afraid that her ashes would get dumped along with a lot of strangers' ashes and it was like sending Mother off UPS. I like the idea of scattering her ashes over the Pacific Ocean. Maybe that is because that is what they did for Donald Douglas, the founder of Douglas Aircraft, after he died although his ashes were dropped from a Douglas DC-3 airplane. Carl suggested we all go out in his sailboat and scatter her ashes in Santa Monica Bay where she loved to swim from the beach in front of lifeguard tower #26 to a red buoy a half mile out. Lisa told Carl that her husband, Todd, gets seasick and that her son, Adam, is afraid of boats and she definitely wanted this to be a positive experience for Adam. I am not sure how scattering his dead grandmother's ashes could ever be a positive experience. Usually Carl lets Lisa have her way, but this time he held his ground. Stephanie suggested a compromise and we all got together to scatter them into the ocean off the end of the Malibu Pier. It was me, Carl, Lisa, Todd, Adam and mother's best friend, Dana. Carl's two sons who live on the East Coast offered to come out, but Lisa decided that would be too many people. There was a small problem when we tried to choose who would actually throw the ashes off, as they were encapsulated in a biodegradable container provided by Palisades Mortuary. The container is supposed to dissolve in water so we wouldn't be littering the ocean (which is illegal in addition to being bad manners), but only one person could actually throw it off. Both Carl and Lisa wanted to do it, but Stephanie and Dana suggested that I do it and that everyone else throw over some lilies which we had with us and that's what we did. The container was kind of like two pie plates stuck together and we all said a few words about Mother and I tossed it into the water. I'm not a very good thrower and, in the wind, it didn't go as far from the pier as I expected. When it landed it surprised me because it kind of fizzed thousands of bubbles when it dissolved, like an Alka-Seltzer. Stephanie said it was because the container was actually made of sodium-bicarbonate, just like Alka Seltzer.

Los Angeles Times ★★

Does the *LA Times* ever check their obituaries? The *Los Angeles Times* has an obituary page that appears at the end of the third section of the daily paper. For certain famous or well-known people the *Times* will write an editorial obituary and print it. Eight years ago they did one for my father, Stephen Katz, who was a producer of television and worked on many well-known TV shows, after he died in a car crash on the Foothill Freeway. Sadly he had apparently been drinking more than he should. The *Times* obituary was a column about a quarter page high, which is pretty big for someone who isn't a famous actor or a senator. You can look it up online anytime at LATIMES. COM. If the person who dies isn't famous enough that the newspaper wants to make it a story, the family can write and pay for an obituary, kind of like a classified ad. My mother wasn't as famous as my dad was and a few days after she died my stepfather, Carl, was planning on writing one for her and submitting it to the *Times* and he asked me to help. Carl wanted to know what I would like to see in Mother's obituary. That was tough. I thought about it and said that he should mention that Mother had many activities including her artwork and her interest in the teachings of Paul Selig, who is a famous writer, channeler and empath. Carl asked my opinion about whether the obituary should mention my father, Stephen Katz. I said I didn't know. He said that usually only the current husband is mentioned in obituaries, but he would be glad to include him if I would like to see my dad's name there. I didn't really know the best way to answer as my parents had divorced when I was three years old and my father had always been very busy with his work and I didn't see much of him as I grew older, so I said I guess it wasn't necessary to include him. Carl showed me the obituary notice and wanted to know if I approved before he showed it to my sister, Lisa, and then sent it to the *Times*. I said yes.

Sarah Rose Epstein (1965–2020)

Sarah was a bright light that shone for all of those who knew her. Whether it was putting on a last-minute gourmet dinner for a dozen friends, or helping to organize an event for her beloved

Zen Center, Sarah treaded the world as if she were climbing Machu Picchu once again—with confident, eager steps. She was a devoted mother and a lover of the ocean. As an artist her finely crafted soapstone sculptures found their way into the homes of many grateful art lovers and are also in the collections of several museums including the Block Art Museum at Northwestern University where she once studied. Always the optimist, always hopeful even in her last days, Sarah will be thought of and missed by her large circle of friends. Sarah is survived by her loving children, Marcus Katz and Lisa (Todd) Samuelson and her husband, Carl Zimansky. There will be a private ceremony for immediate family. Donations may be sent to the Los Angeles Zen Center and the Autism Society of America.

Carl was just about to email it to Lisa when a friend of his called to say that he had just been reading the *LA Times* online and seen an obituary for Mother already there. Carl thought there must be a mistake, but he pulled up the *Times* online and found this obituary already posted:

Sarah Rose Katz (1965–2020)

Sarah Katz of Santa Monica passed away at Cedars-Sinai Hospital after a heroic battle with pancreatic cancer. Sarah was born in suburban Chicago in 1960 to philanthropists Samuel and Freda Epstein. Samuel was the founder of Honor Jewelers, a chain of jewelry stores that he later sold. After getting a degree in art at Northwestern University, Sarah came to California to practice her painting and sculpture in 1964 and found employment in the scenic department of 20th Century Fox studios. It was there that she met a young director named Stephen Katz and married him soon after and together they had two children, Marcus and Lisa. Although they separated, Sarah and Stephen stayed in touch, and Stephen went on to create the popular reality television show *The Cream of Beverly Hills* before his tragic and untimely death. Sarah enjoyed most her two wonderful and loving grandchildren, Adam and Elizabeth, from devoted daughter Lisa Samuelson and her husband, Todd. Sarah had recently been married to Carl Zimansky. There will be a private ceremony. Donations in her name may be sent to the American Cancer Society.

Carl was very upset that Lisa had written it without consulting him and that both he and I had been barely mentioned. Also Mother had always used her family name, Epstein, after her divorce from my father, not Katz and not even Zimanksy, Carl's last name. Carl couldn't understand why the *Los Angeles Times* saw fit to publish the obituary without consulting him. He said that he was not going to call Lisa right away because he needed to cool down and he didn't think there was any sense in sending a revised obituary to the *Los Angeles Times*, but he did send the one he composed to the *Chicago Tribune* and you can see it there if you look online. If the *Los Angeles Times* will publish an obituary from anyone who submits one and pays the price (very expensive by the way) then I don't think they are being appropriately respectful of the family of the deceased. I am not criticizing the way they report news, but they should change their policy and verify that the obituary comes from the spouse first, and, if not, from all of the children together.

Dr. Renee DeSantis ★ ★

Right now I am angry with my therapist, Dr. DeSantis. At my last session I showed her some of my recent postings, especially about my sister, Lisa, and how she hijacked my mother's obituary notice from my stepfather. Dr. DeSantis has asked me to stop Yelping. She says that I am making public too much information that should remain private and that I should at least pause my postings or at least not speak publicly so much about my family and my intimate feelings. She says she is concerned that something bad will come from it and I will regret it. This is surprising when she was the one who first encouraged me to post with my complaint about Barrington Farms playing loud trumpet music. A big part of my treatment was to make me feel better about myself and, to use an expression of Dr. DeSantis, "empowered." I have received 13 "useful" votes, 18 "funny" and 7 "cool" so clearly people appreciate what I do. I have been IM'd many times by people saying how much they enjoy my posts. That is definitely empowering! I don't think I have anything to hide, although I don't think I'll show my reviews to Dr. DeSantis anymore but I wonder if she will bother to look them up.

Update to My Dr. DeSantis Review ★ ★ ★ ★ ★

I am sorry I gave Dr. DeSantis a two-star review yesterday. I was angry after seeing her in my weekly session when she asked me to pause my Yelping. In fairness, let me first say that not long ago I would have given Dr. DeSantis five stars. Before I saw Dr. DeSantis I had seen seven other therapists and psychiatrists relating to my autism spectrum disorder. Dr. DeSantis, who is a psychiatrist and a medical doctor who specializes in treating people on the spectrum, was the only one who didn't treat me as if I had a disease, but rather as if I was just a different kind of thinker than the average person. I can't help that others feel uncomfortable in the presence of someone like me who has difficulty picking up emotional cues, is socially awkward and has difficulty responding with appropriate facial expressions and tends to speak in a monotone. There are two ways to help a person like me. Dr. DeSantis helped me with both. The first is to try to make them feel comfortable with who they are and to not feel bad if they are shunned by others. The real weakness is in the neurotypical person who is not able to see another's true worth. The other, to be most honest, is to help you "fake it" so that you seem more neurotypical to them and therefore they will treat you more like one of them. It doesn't mean changing who you are. I think it's more like a disguise that would allow you to travel in a foreign country without being treated as an outsider. There are exercises that you can do to help you make eye contact and to inflect your voice in a more neurotypical way. And Dr. DeSantis also has been helping me to deal with the death of my mother. I am grateful to her for that. I still do not agree with her about posting to Yelp, however.

NKLA Pet Adoption Center ★ ★ ★ ★ ★

After Mother died in April, my step-dad, Carl, came to me and told me that the one good thing that might come from losing mother was that now I could have a dog if I wanted. That was quite a surprise. He knew I had asked Mother on several occasions if we could get a dog. Mother was allergic to dogs, and even though I live upstairs in the garage apartment behind our house, she was concerned that the dog would somehow get into the house. Carl said that he had always had a dog when he was growing up, and he often wished that I could have one. A week after the funeral, Carl went with me to NKLA shelter. The "NK" stands for no kill and "LA" is for Los Angeles. It is in West Los Angeles near the 405 freeway and, unlike the city dog shelters, it is not so sad. When you go in it looks new and clean and kind of like the lobby of a Sheraton hotel. Everybody wears team blue polo shirts with NKLA on the pockets and they ask you right away what kind of pet you are looking for. I have heard that some really rich animal lover started it. They rescue cats as well as dogs, but I am not a fan of cats. I thought a lot the night before about what kind of dog I might want. I decided I would like a medium size dog that has some fur, but doesn't shed too much. There are several nice kennel areas where you can view the dogs. Some of the dogs look happy and glad to see you, some of them bark and snarl, and some of them are sad and sit at the back of their cage. The dogs are mostly mutts, but there are also poodles and pit bulls and Chihuahuas and Labradors and just all kinds of dogs. I know people wonder why there aren't as many different breeds of humans as there are of dogs, but people confuse "race" and "breed." Breeding is done on purpose to dogs by humans who are trying to isolate a particular breed type. Also dogs can reproduce after they are a year old, where people take much longer before they have babies, usually about 20 years. In the same time period that humans have 4000 generations, dogs can have 40,000, so ten times the opportunities to change. When I saw Sadie I right away knew she was the dog for me. The sign on the cage said she was a mixed terrier. She had gray and white fur (they call it salt and pepper), but it is the kind of fur that doesn't shed. She was hanging out in the back of her cage looking awfully scared, but when I put my hand through the wire, she came up to me to lick it. At NKLA if you say you are interested in a particular dog they will bring it into a separate little room so you can get acquainted. I LOVED Sadie from the second I saw her. Maybe it was because she was a little reserved and a little shy like me. Carl asked me if she was the "one" and I surprised myself by giving a big "yes" right away. I had to fill out a form to show you will be a responsible owner. Carl paid them $248 which covered her spaying and licensing. I know my mother has left me some money of my own, actually quite a lot, so I would rather have paid it myself, but the money hadn't come through yet and I told Carl I would be sure to pay him back.

Jonathan's Steam Cleaning ★ ★ ★ ★ ★

As I recently lost a close family member, I haven't been posting on Yelp as often as I intended, but I hope to post much more now. There are some Yelpers with several hundred reviews and, from my research, the record for most reviews in the Los Angeles metropolitan area is 3,768 as of today by Frank Chen of Laguna, California. He has been posting for seven years, which translates to 10.35 posts a week. I will try to post at least that many each week and maybe someday, if Frank slows down, I can break his record. On to the review of Jonathan's. My new dog, Sadie, pooped on my carpet. I had made her a bed on the floor of my bedroom out of an old blanket and I heard her kind of whimpering in the night, so I got up to see if she was all right and I accidentally stepped in it. Gross! I am very sensitive to strong smells but I am good at breathing through my mouth. Later I took a really long hot shower with lots of soap. The next morning I called NKLA, the pet adoption agency, and Vickie there said that Sadie was definitely trained to poop outside, but if a dog is very nervous about their new surroundings they can get confused. I know I would be nervous if suddenly some person I didn't know yanked me off to a strange house. I hope this doesn't happen again, although I will probably forgive her if it does. She is a very sweet dog and likes to lick my hand like it was made of candy. Today I called Jonathan's Steam Cleaning because of their 47 five and four-star Yelp reviews and Jonathan himself came over a few hours later. Jonathan has a steam hose that reaches all the way to his truck that was parked in the driveway and he cleaned everything up. Jonathan said that about half his business is because of pets. He offered to spray some deodorant on the carpet, but I don't like the perfume smell. The poop odor seems to be all gone and my rug is clean. In fact, my rug is cleaner than it has been for years.

Chinois Restaurant ★ ★ ★ ★ ★

Yei jiàn hěn bàng de canting! (That means "great restaurant" in Mandarin.) Yesterday was my twenty-second birthday and my step-dad, Carl, walked down the driveway from the main house to my apartment and asked if I'd like to do anything special for my birthday. My mother, who recently died, used to make me a coconut birthday cake. I asked instead if he could take me to a nice restaurant because I know that if Carl made me a coconut cake we would both wind up sad and if we went to a nice restaurant I could have a great meal and also be able write a new Yelp review. I told him of my plan to have as many posts as Frank Chen and to become a Yelp Elite. He said that sounded like a good idea, but I should probably just take it one post at a time. Carl has told me before about how important it is to "live in the moment." Carl and my mother were only married for a year when she got her cancer eighteen months ago, but I think they really did try to live in the moment. Before they were married they traveled to Morocco and Nepal together and even surfed in Portugal. Carl asked if I would like to go to Chinois for my birthday, a very special restaurant on Main Street. It is run by the famous chef Wolfgang Puck. We all went there once last year with my sister, Lisa, her husband, Todd, and my little niece, Elizabeth. I ordered their Shanghai lobster, which is lobster in a curry sauce and it is what they call a "signature" dish. I know that there are 438 reviews already on Yelp for Chinois and it has a five-star average rating so they don't really need my review, but this is a good opportunity to reach new readers by reviewing a more upscale restaurant. Carl told me that Mother had left some money for me, so maybe in the future I will be able to eat in fancier restaurants and review them. Not that I would choose expensive restaurants exclusively, just sometimes. Carl invited Lisa and Todd to come, but Lisa said that she had office work to catch up on. She did send me a birthday card, one of those dateline ones that tell you all the important things that happened the year I was born, 1994. According to the card, that was the year that OJ was arrested for having killed Nicole Simpson. That happened about two miles from our house, although I was just born then, so I didn't know about it at the time. Also someone named Newt Gingrich was named speaker of the House of Representatives.

Carl said to order whatever I wanted, so I had the crab cake appetizer and then the Shanghai Lobster. The crab cakes were small, but very crisp and had lots of real crab in them, not like the frozen kind from the market that is all filler. They came with a very sweet dipping sauce, maybe a bit too sweet, but with a lot of different flavors that made me wonder how they made it. The lobster is served so that it looks like a King's crown. It's already taken apart with the shell placed around it on the plate and the pieces are in the center with this delicious curry sauce mixed in with rice. I had a creepy thought—how would a famous cannibal chef arrange a meal of me on a plate? (That's a joke.) The waiter brought out a big piece of chocolate lava cake with vanilla ice cream on the side and a candle burning in the middle. Red syrup drizzled around the edges of the plate spelled out "Happy Birthday Marcus." Carl handed me an envelope with a Simpsons birthday card inside featuring Mr. Burns (my favorite Simpsons character) saying "This personal birthday sentiment has been brought to you by the Springfield Nuclear Power Plant. Providing safe, clean and efficient energy for a happy, healthy, and productive community. Your pay will be docked for the time it took to read this card." There were two one hundred dollar bills inside. Carl said I shouldn't deposit it, but be reckless and buy something I wouldn't ordinarily get. Reckless doesn't come easy to me, but I will try to follow his advice. Next week I have to go with Carl to a bank where someone in their trust department is the trustee of Mother's estate so that we can talk about money things.

Petco ★★★★★

Sam at NKLA animal shelter had suggested that we get a crate for Sadie, my new dog. I didn't know what she meant and pictured a wooden box, but she showed me a crate that they had there and it is just a sort of wire cage. Sam said that to many people it looks like dog jail, but not to dogs. If you train your dog to be in the crate, they will feel very secure in there and soon would rather be in it than outside of it. I think in a way I understand that. I know that I prefer to be in a corner of my room by the bed and I put a chair and a basket of clothes in front of me there so that I have a space within the space.

Sam said it is also very comforting for dogs if you need to leave them at home and also you will know that your dog is secure and not damaging anything. So far, except for pooping on the floor once when she was new, Sadie is very respectful of all of my belongings. After talking with the salesperson at Petco I decided to get a 36-inch crate with two doors—one for Sadie to get in and out of and one to get at the water and food bowls. You don't want to get a crate that is either too big or too small. I also got some True Chews Premium Dog Treats which they recommended to give to Sadie when she sat in the crate. When we got home I put dog food and water in a bowl in the crate and at first she didn't want to go in, but then she did and now she seems to like it. Then I gave her a True Chew and she jumped up and was happy. I think this will all work out. The crate was on sale and only cost $36.99 plus $3.72 tax.

Beach Café at Casa Cabana Hotel
(Pico Boulevard Stop #1) ★ ★

They should call it "Bleach Café" because everything is white—the walls, the tables and the china. I know I must sound like some kind of a rich hipster because my last restaurant review was for upscale Chinois Restaurant and now I'm reviewing another fancy place, Beach Café at Casa Cabana Hotel at Santa Monica Beach. But the reason I went to Chinois was because my stepfather, Carl, took me out for a special birthday dinner. Beach Café, with its $25 hamburgers, is not a place I would regularly go to. But it's all part of my *grand new plan* that I am about to reveal to you. Are you ready? I owe this idea to one of my heroes (not Deadpool or any superhero as you might expect if you know me) but Jonathan Gold, the Los Angeles restaurant critic (and the only restaurant critic to win a Pulitzer Prize) who died recently. In 1989, when he was in his twenties like me, Mr. Gold decided that he would dine his way up Pico Boulevard which is fifteen and a half miles long and goes through many ethnic neighborhoods lined with literally hundreds of restaurants. I don't know why they call it "Pico" which means "small" in Spanish if it is fifteen and a half miles long. Beginning his journey at a Salvadoran pupuseria downtown on Pico near Main Street, he planned to make his way west to the beach in Santa Monica. He went to a new restaurant almost every day and he made himself strict rules to follow. I like rules, too, which is probably part of why I like the plan. He said he would have to eat at every restaurant on Pico and a "restaurant" was any place that served prepared food at a table or counter. If they were closed when he arrived, he would move on to the next restaurant, but return on the next day they were open. I decided that in honor of Mr. Gold, I would eat my way down Pico Boulevard, but in reverse—west to east starting with Beach Café instead of east to west. I will report all of my findings here on Yelp, good or bad. I promise all my readers that my restaurant reviews will be absolutely honest, and that I will try to be open to all types of restaurants and all kinds of cuisines. But $25 for a hamburger? $10 for an ear of corn on the side? And that's just for lunch. Oops. I guess I just prejudged. But a dinner with dessert and no wine is easily over $100 a person. Solution? Happy hour from 4–6 p.m.! Drinking alcohol interferes too much with my thinking, but sliders, tacos and fried calamari don't, so no need to order a pricey mixed drink. On to my review! There were no parking spaces around and I was forced to bring Atomic Betty, my 1984 Mercedes into the driveway where four valets in white uniforms were waiting and a turquoise Lamborghini was conspicuously parked out front, probably to show off how they have rich customers. When I asked how much they charge for parking, the valet just wrote my license plate number on a ticket without even answering as he opened my door and pointed to a sign that said $9. A group of three really pretty young women all dressed up and in spike heels giggled on their way in the front door, looking at me the same way that the valet looked at my old car. Inside I found a table in a corner away from the bar that was noisy and crowded and everybody was dressed up. I ordered a fish taco, fried calamari and a Perrier. It cost $22 plus tip. They grilled the tiny scrap of white fish instead of battering and frying it in the classic Ensenada style that I like best. If you are going to grill the fish, it should be a nice, fresh piece of fish and this wasn't. The tortilla was store-bought, rubbery and tasteless. There was American sour cream (not real Mexican crema), watery pico de gallo, a sprig of cilantro, and a chunk of lime. It wasn't even in the same league as Tacos Baja Ensenada, my favorite place for fish tacos. The calamari, however, were crispy and better, and possibly worth the $7 happy hour price. Two stars are all you get, Beach Café. The Yelper of doom has spoken!

Santa Monica Museum of Flying ★ ★ ★ ★ ★

Thanks to all who voted my other reviews so far as "funny" or "cool." I think that Yelping comes naturally to me and pretty soon I'm going to have hundreds, and then thousands of useful Yelps and hopefully be invited to Elite. I will continue my Pico Boulevard Yelp reviews, plus wherever else I might go that merits reviewing. I hope you will support me on this. Also, if you are currently a Yelp Elite, please think about recommending me for Elite status, if not, now, perhaps later when I have proven myself more.

For full disclosure I need to say that I am a docent on Saturdays at the Museum of Flying in Santa Monica. I got the job (it's volunteer, so they actually don't pay me) and although it is a very small museum, not nearly as big as the Planes of Fame Museum in Chino, for example, it is well located on historic Clover Field, which was famous lately because Harrison Ford (Mr. Han Solo) crashed his classic 1942 Ryan PT-22 Recruit trainer on the golf course at the end of the runway. Everyone said it was great piloting to bring the plane down on the golf course and not injure anyone on the ground. I think it is what you might expect of Han Solo. I have never met Mr. Ford in person, but I have seen both the Cessna 525 and the Waco Biplane take off and I hope Mr. Han Solo was at the controls when they did, although I was too far away to tell. It is also where Donald Douglas and the Douglas Corporation factory built the famous DC-3 and the WWII army version of the DC-3 called the C-47. Before I ever got there they also included some other non-Douglas planes like an F86 and a Lockheed Vega to spice things up. Some people say the Douglas DC-3 is the most airworthy and sturdiest passenger plane ever made. They are still flown all around the world even at seventy years old. Nobody really knows how long a DC-3 can last if properly maintained. They built them before there were computers to compute structure loads so, to be safe, they just way overbuilt. The most popular thing in the museum is not a DC-3, however. It is an actual cockpit pulled from a decommissioned Federal Express Boeing 727. You can operate the real controls. The museum gives you an official laminated preflight pilot's checklist so that you know what buttons to press and levers to pull and when. I have done it at least a dozen times myself. I happened to be standing near the 727 when an eight-year-old, who was sitting in the pilot's seat looking confused, asked his mother what a "trim tab" was. She said she was sorry but didn't know. I told him that it was just a little movable flap on the surface of the wing that the pilot can adjust so that when he is flying he doesn't have to work to keep the plane level. The mother asked me if I wouldn't mind helping her son with the rest so I sat in the copilot's seat next to him. After we finished our simulated "takeoff" I explained to them how Clover Field is a really historic place and also about how in 1924 two Douglas ST1 converted torpedo planes flown by pilots from the U.S. Army Air Service (this was before there was an Air Force) were the very first airplanes to circumnavigate the world. Lt. Erik Nelson and Lt. Lowell Smith were the pilots but the circumnavigation was a team effort. When the boy and his mother had to leave the mother thanked me and handed me a ten dollar bill. I told her that she had already paid when she entered but she said that the money was just for me. I didn't want to take it as I didn't really need the money, but she insisted, saying that they both learned a lot and that it was only fair for me to be paid. After they left, Scott, the museum manager, walked over to me. I was afraid he was going to ask me to give the ten dollars back. Instead he said that he overheard me and was impressed by how much I knew about Douglas Aviation. He then asked if I would be interested in being a docent and talking to more visitors about the museum's planes. I said that I would be most interested in talking to people about Douglas airplanes and not so much the others as Douglas is the real reason for the museum being here. He said that would be fine and asked if when I talk to people that I try to talk a little slower. It is true that when I get wound up talking about aviation I can talk a little too fast. I agreed to come between 11 a.m. and 4 p.m. on Saturdays. They put out a whole box of good doughnuts for the employees and volunteers from Number One Doughnuts, my favorite doughnut shop. I will review Number One later and have a surprise for you when I do. I am giving the Museum of Flying four stars. You might probably expect me to give it five stars just because I do work there, but if fellow Yelpers are ever going to trust me on Yelp I promise to be completely honest and neutral as much as possible. They are very kind people who run it and they work hard to keep the museum clean and up to date with limited financing, but I wish they would concentrate more on the Douglas history and less about other aviation companies.

Cha Cha Chicken (Pico Boulevard Stop #2) ★ ★ ★ ★ ★

Day-o! Day-o! We gonna get you some real Caribbean food at Cha Cha Chicken on Pico Boulevard right by the beach, Bruddah! It be #2 on my Jonathan Gold memorial Pico Boulevard crawl, Mon! Whatchou think? You like the jerk chicken and the dirty rice, Mon? Me too! Cha Cha Chicken is a happy place, where you order at the window and sit in a crazily painted outdoor patio and they bring your food to you after you sit down. Everybody is nice and friendly and makes sure you get what you want. They refill your soda for free. I got black bean soup and Cha Cha Chicken, white meat with dirty rice, black beans and medium hot sauce. The jerk sauce is really savory and good. Maybe the chicken is better in Jamaica, but for Santa Monica, this seems pretty good and you save on plane fare.

Steve Shelton Reality Appraisals ★ ★ ★ ★

When I got home from my job at the Santa Monica Library today I saw a big new Mercedes sedan parked in our driveway. I could see through a side window of the house that my stepfather, Carl, was in the living room talking to a man in a business suit. Twenty minutes later Carl came to the door of my apartment over the garage with the same man. Carl introduced him as Steve Shelton and said he was a real estate appraiser. He said that the trustees of Mother's trust had asked him to see how much they could sell the house for. As you can imagine, I found the idea of selling the house pretty upsetting. How would you feel if it was the house you grew up in? Maybe I was being mean, but I told Carl I didn't want Steve Shelton to come in. Carl said that it was important that Steve be able to take a look at the apartment because the bank needed an appraisal of the entire property, but then Steve looked over my shoulder into my apartment and said that if I was uncomfortable with it, it wouldn't be necessary. He said that he had already seen all he really needed to see in the main house and that from what he could see of my apartment it looked very nice and especially clean. I appreciate that he was just doing his job and he respected my privacy. I still have hopes that the house may not be sold, but thanks to Steve Shelton for staying cool and not making me more upset than I already am.

Bigbowl Lanes (Pico Boulevard Stop #3) ★

Bigbowl! Badeat! I am really trying to be true to Jonathan Gold's Pico Boulevard credo as I work my way up Pico Boulevard, and eating in every restaurant on my route. After going to Bigbowl I have decided that this may be harder than I thought. It's not an old style bowling alley like when I was little. When I was a child this used to be Santa Monica Bowl and then there was a sweet little café next door. That was before Bigbowl, a national chain took it over. When you open the door you are blasted with loud pop music. I mean really, really, really loud, so you would have to yell to be heard by a person standing (or bowling) next to you. And it's jam-packed with people bowling and waiting to bowl. There are flashing video games all around making even more loud noise, and a booze-smelling bar area off the main room with a big sports TV. Did I say how loud it is? And what kind of food do you think people who like music this loud eat? Maybe you would guess chicken wings, ribs and greasy pizza? Or how about stuffing your face with a two-foot long hot dog off a shiny oversized menu with giant photos? Maybe you would like to ignore this review because I didn't actually eat anything here. I spent about thirty seconds inside the door and then I left.

Bel Ami Group Home ★ ★

My sister, Lisa, who has a different last name from me (Samuelson) because she is married, texted that she wanted to visit me. I know she is very busy and she rarely comes to see me. When she got here I introduced her to Sadie and she gave her a pat on her back (Sadie prefers to be petted on the top of her head) and said Sadie is very cute but that having a dog is a big responsibility. Lisa often tells me things that I already know. Like a lot of people, she acts like Asperger's is somehow related to being stupid. In fact Aspies are statistically of medium to high intelligence. I won't tell you what I am. I will let you decide. Lisa wanted me to go for a ride in her car with her. I asked if we could bring Sadie. She has a big Volvo SUV and there is plenty of room in the back, but Lisa said no because she was afraid Sadie would shed on the upholstery, which, of course she wouldn't. I decided staying home would be a good test of how Sadie does left alone in her crate, so I said okay and I left Sadie with extra water. She barked as I went to the door, but I gave her a treat and petted her and she quieted down and Lisa and I left. I didn't like leaving Sadie, but I know I can't be with her every minute even if I would like to. I asked Lisa where we were going and she said she had something she wanted to show me and that she thought I would like it. As she drove us onto the 405 Freeway and in the direction of the San Fernando Valley she said that we needed to have a serious talk. She said that Mother left a trust for us which is kind of like a will and it says that the house has to be sold and both Carl and I will have to move. Of course I already knew that because a man had come by several days ago to appraise the house. I said that didn't seem fair to make me move and it didn't sound like Mother to want me to do that. She said it was written into the trust and nobody could do anything about it. I asked if Carl and I could move someplace together and she said that she expects Carl will probably go off adventuring like he used to, maybe sailing to Tahiti or on one of his mountain climbing trips. She said that life would be changing a lot for me and that I needed a new place to live. I foolishly asked if she was maybe thinking I should move in with her which would have probably been a bad idea. They have a really big house with a pool in Encino, in the San Fernando Valley. She said that she didn't think I would be happy in her house and for once I think she was right. She said that she had looked around and had found a very good place for me that she was sure I would like. I asked where it was and she said it was in Van Nuys. I don't want to be a snob, but Van Nuys is not Santa Monica. It is hotter and tackier and farther from the beach. If I absolutely had to move I needed to at least be close to my own neighborhood. I know the stores and the people and everything. Lisa said that although I could take care of myself in many ways, I still needed someone to watch out for me and that there was a place in Van Nuys where I could live with other people who had disabilities similar to mine and where there was a person in charge who would look after us. It is called a group home. I didn't think I would want to live with strangers and I certainly didn't want to live in Van Nuys. Also I don't like the term "disability" when other people say it. I asked how many people live in the home and she said four plus the person who watches over us. I told her I didn't want a stranger saying what I can do. Lisa started to enunciate her words as if I am a five year old. She does that when I disagree with her. And she starts speaking louder. I asked how much money there is and she said that she really didn't want to talk about money, but what is best for me. The Google Maps voice told us to exit the 405 at Burbank Boulevard and then we made a left on Sepulveda and a right on Hazeltine and then a left on Martha Street. Then Google said we were at our destination. Not a very pretty street. Not at all like Marguerita Street in Santa Monica which has a big tree canopy and green shrubs and flowers. You could hear the trucks rumbling from the 405 Freeway three blocks away. The house had two stories covered with dirty tan stucco and it didn't have any landscaping except for a couple of half-dead oleanders. At the door there was a little metal plaque over the doorbell that said "Bel Ami Residence" and "Groupcare United Partners LLC." Another sign said "Private. No Solicitors." In England a solicitor is what they call a lawyer. I don't think they meant "no lawyers." That's a joke, but there is no laugh emoji in Yelp reviews. Lisa rang the bell and a woman came to the door and said her name was Kristin. Kristin said she was the resident counselor and had been expecting us and to come in. In fairness Kristin seemed perfectly polite and nice. A really skinny man maybe about sixty with no shirt on was sitting on a recliner in the living room watching *The Price is Right* on TV, which is a show I don't like very much. Kristin brought me in and introduced him to me. His name was Albert, but when I said hello he just kept watching TV where they were playing the "Magic Number" game in which a woman had to guess a price that was between the price of a set of Regal Cookware and Weber Barbecue. Kristin wanted to show us the rest of the house. Besides the kitchen and dining room there were three bedrooms upstairs and one downstairs that Kristin said was Albert's because he had trouble with stairs and two bathrooms, one upstairs and one downstairs. Kristin said that Albert's not allowed to hog the downstairs one just because he has the ground floor bedroom. When we started up the stairs to see what she said would be my room, was when the real trouble started. I asked Kristin if Sadie could stay in my room with me and Kristin asked who Sadie was and I told her that Sadie was my dog and she said that she was sorry but they don't allow dogs there, not at all. Of course that made me very upset and I didn't even want to see the bedroom. When Lisa said I should just look at it I started pacing which everybody who knows about the spectrum can tell you often leads to a meltdown so Lisa tried to calm me down, but she is not very talented at calming anyone, let alone someone on the spectrum. First she said we could find a nice family to take Sadie. When I said that I wasn't going to go anywhere without Sadie she said that because Mother died that things have to change and we have to get used to it. She said that she couldn't take Sadie because Todd, her husband, is allergic to dogs, but she is sure that Carl would take him and I could visit Sadie whenever I wanted. But she had just said how Carl is always off on a trip someplace, on climbing expeditions or something and you can't take Sadie to Kathmandu. I asked Lisa why I couldn't just find another place near the house on Marguerita where I could stay by myself with Sadie and she said that Mother didn't provide for that in her will and that there wasn't enough money to keep me forever in an apartment in Santa Monica and almost no apartments will allow dogs and she didn't want to be the one responsible for me if I was in an apartment on my own. Normally if I am having a meltdown I try to fight it by thinking hard about something very specific like making a list of the parts (infusor, bladed gear, steel gear, etc.) I will need to find how to complete the machine to help me to escape from the cemetery on level 13 of Legend of Grimrock. There are 22 parts in all. Or I can think of the names of all of the fighter planes flown by the Luftwaffe between 1933 and 1945. I have also tried to imagine a complete flight on Flight Simulator from takeoff to landing, preferably on a classic biplane like the Lockheed Vega or the Waco YMF. But I didn't feel like calming myself down so I didn't bother. I wound up a screaming mess on the floor in the hallway on the second floor and that didn't go well with Kristin. I don't know if Kristin even wanted me there after that which was okay with me. In the car on the way home Lisa said I had the meltdown on purpose, but I didn't, even if I didn't try as hard as I could to stop it. I didn't like Bel Ami. I don't want to have to live with other people. Maybe it's okay for some people and maybe this review isn't totally fair, but my Yelp isn't anybody else's Yelp and I wouldn't want to live there. The only good thing for me about this whole episode is that this review happens to be the first review for Bel Ami Group Home and I have learned that Yelp gives special credit for adding first reviews when they consider someone for Elite status.

Bravo Café (Pico Boulevard Stop #4) ★ ★ ★ ★

No meat. No problem. It is amazing to me that a cute little vegan café can exist just a few steps from the noise and oversize two-foot hot dogs of Bigbowl Lanes (Pico Stop #3). I'm not a vegan, or a vegetarian, but I like a good salad and Avo Café's Farmers' Market Mista is just that. Spinach, arugula, avocado, grated carrots, cucumbers and sprouts is like the antidote to a Behemoth Burger at Bigbowl Lanes next door. I had a Farmer's Salad for lunch with a berry banana smoothie and I felt like I was doing my body and my taste buds a favor. I ordered at the counter from Jennifer, who was really cute with blonde hair and a pony tail. I tried to chat her up because I think it would be very good for me to have a very healthy girlfriend someday who would inspire me to eat well all the time and help me lose a few pounds and get in shape. Dr. DeSantis and I have talked about this kind of situation before so I didn't want to be inappropriate. Dr. DeSantis says that acting the right way with women is even a big problem for neurotypical men and it is no wonder that it is a problem for me. If you are a neurotypical person you may be thinking "Why doesn't he just act normal?" I would say to that, if you are a regular neurotypical man, why don't you just always act cool like George Clooney or Brad Pitt all the time? It's not so easy, is it? I asked her if she was going to school and where she lived because my mother and Dr. DeSantis both have told me it's better to ask people questions than just go on talking about yourself which might make people think you are narcissistic, but unfortunately she said she was busy getting orders out and couldn't talk right then, but she was very polite. If I ever finish my Pico Boulevard eating odyssey I would like to come back again to Bravo Café and I hope Jennifer is still here.

Northwestern Trust Bank ★ ★ ★ ★ ★

I probably should not be reviewing Northwestern Trust Bank for two good reasons. First is that I have only been there for a first meeting. Second is that both my stepfather, Carl, and my sister, Lisa, say I should not be writing about something so private in a public forum like Yelp. But if my opinion (which is very positive) of Northwestern Trust changes later I will just update my review. Also, I have noticed that the most popular Yelp reviews are the ones that tell you the most about the person writing. Like when Alice S. talked about her personal experiences with having received a badly designed prosthetic arm in her reviews and complained that it became nearly impossible for her to operate a Redbox. Or when Jerryonestar wrote about how he was refused service at his own uncle's restaurant because of a family feud and how his brother later threw a brick in the restaurant window. Anyway, while there are, no doubt, some things I expect to keep private, I will try to be as open as I can. I think that is a path to Yelp Elite status along with making sure I write lots of reviews. As those of you who follow my reviews know, my mother died and is selling her house and now I will have to move. When my sister tried to have me go to a group home, I had a meltdown. I told my stepfather, Carl, about how my sister tried to make me go to a group home even though I didn't want to because she said there wasn't enough money for me to stay in an apartment forever and he suggested that we both talk with the trustee of Mother's estate. I asked if Lisa had to go with us and he said she didn't if I didn't want her. Carl made an appointment on Tuesday at 10 a.m. at Northwestern Trust Bank which, according to him, is the trustee of the estate. I had already been told by Carl that the estate had been divided to go 50% to me, 30% to my sister, Lisa, probably because she and her husband Todd have plenty of money of their own, 15% to Carl who was Mother's husband (and my stepfather) for two years until she died, and 5% to the Los Angeles Zen Center. I won't say how much there was because that would be crossing a line of privacy, but mother inherited quite a lot of money from my grandparents and there is still a considerable amount left. The bank is in an office building in Century City but it's on the thirtieth floor and it doesn't look like a bank. There are no tellers or ATMs like Wells Fargo where I bank. The trust officer we met was named Emma Reese. She welcomed Carl and me and said that she was sorry that Lisa said she couldn't make it to this meeting. She told me about what her job was as a trustee and asked if I had any questions. The first thing I asked her was if I could live in an apartment in my neighborhood or if I had to go to a group home. Emma said that as far as she knew I had a right to make my own decisions about living conditions because there was no custodianship set up for me. Also she said there should be enough income from the trust to permit me to live in a moderately priced apartment for as long as I like. That was really good news and different from what my sister, Lisa, told me. Emma explained that Mother had arranged for me to have a monthly allowance of $7000. That was quite a surprise, as before Mother died I lived mostly on $1047 a month from SSDI (Social Security Disability Insurance) based on my diagnosis of autism and because my father had died. My SSDI check goes directly into my Wells Fargo checking account on the second Wednesday of every month, but of course a lot of my expenses were already paid for by Mother and I didn't have to pay any rent on the apartment in the garage behind our house, so I have always put a regular amount every month into my savings account and I use the rest for clothes and books and computer games and food. Ms. Reese explained that I would be expected to be responsible for all of my bills now, but I didn't have to worry because there was more money which could be available in case I had medical expenses or wanted to go on a special trip or I had some other important need for money but I would have to submit the expenses to her office. She said it was her job to make sure the money lasted for as long as I needed it. Carl told Ms. Reese that I have always been very responsible with money and she needn't worry. Also Ms. Reese told me that my therapist, Dr. DeSantis, would continue to be paid directly by the bank from my trust fund. I am glad I probably won't have to worry about money for the rest of my life which is good because I don't think I am very good at earning it. She then explained that the trust agreement said that Mother's house on Marguerita Street would be sold which I sadly already knew and both Carl and I will have to find new places to live. Carl said he was planning to move back onto his boat and I could stay with him for a short while if I needed a temporary place, and he would help me find an apartment. This was all quite a lot to take in, but I felt better knowing Emma Reese was on my side. As we left, she put her hand on my shoulder (the touch bothers me, but I have learned to put up with it because I know people mean well) and said that the Northwestern Trust never can replace a family member, but that I could let her know whenever I had a problem having to do with money and they would try to always act in my best interests. Also she gave me a new Northwestern Trust checkbook with my name on it. On the elevator down, Carl told me he would probably move back onto his boat when our house is sold and I was welcome stay there for a short time until I found an apartment, but we needed to find one right away and figure out what to do with the furniture in the house and Mother's clothes and belongings. I'd rather not think about it, but I guess I have to. I will see Dr. DeSantis three times this week and that will help.

West LA Rentals ★ ★ ★ ★

After my really bad experience at Bel Ami group home it was clear I needed to find a new apartment. My monthly income is $7000 plus my SSDI of $1047 which equals $8047. I am very big on research so I checked on CNBC.com, Creditkarma.com, quora.com and other budget websites and they agree that an apartment should cost 30% of a person's income. That meant an apartment for me should cost $2414. I wouldn't be able to find an apartment that was exactly $2414 (if I did that would be like a magic sign and I should rent it right away). I didn't know a rental agent, but where better than Yelp to get a recommendation? I contacted Amy Rosenberg at West LA Rentals to help me find a place. She had an aggregate 4.5 star rating with lots of comments about her being very friendly and helpful. I didn't know if $2414 was a lot or a little for an apartment, but when I met with Amy at her office I showed her my list of minimum requirements.

1. *In Santa Monica,* preferably near Mother's old house on Marguerita Avenue so I don't have to change grocery stores and drug stores where the employees know me. Also I wanted to be able to walk by my old house and remind myself of how things used to be. After having two extra sessions with Dr. DeSantis, we agree that, considering how much change has come to my life already, it would be good for me to stay in familiar surroundings.
2. *Quiet.* Not on a main street. No noisy neighbors. No musicians or people who play their televisions loud.
3. *Accepts dogs.* Sadie is very well behaved and doesn't bark much.
4. *Parking space* for Atomic Betty, my 1984 Mercedes. (Room to open doors without chipping the paint.)
5. *No wood floors.* The cracks between the boards collect dirt and germs and are very distracting to look at when I am sitting in a chair and looking down.
6. *Has its own washing machine and dryer.* Some people think it is all right to wash their clothes in a laundromat where other people have already washed their dirty underwear, but not me.

Amy asked if I preferred a one bedroom or a studio. I didn't know what the difference was, but she explained that a studio has the bed in the living room. My apartment at home had a separate cozy bedroom which I liked. She asked how much Sadie weighed as some apartments only allow smaller dogs. I wanted to know what she meant by "smaller dog" and she said usually it means under 25 pounds. Fortunately Sadie had been weighed at NKLA when I got her and she weighed 14 pounds, although she might have gained a little weight because she has a good appetite. Amy said that she knew of apartments available, but finding one that allowed Sadie and had its own washer and dryer would be difficult in my price range. She said that Santa Monica is one of the most expensive and difficult places to find housing because so many people want to live on the Westside. A lot of them are young people who work for Google and Facebook and Snapchat and make a lot of money and they have been driving up the price of rents. What amounts to 30% of my income might only be 10% for them. Then she showed me on her computer what was available in Santa Monica and there were only two apartments that allowed dogs and had a washer and dryer. They were both one bedroom units not far from the beach. One cost $3750 a month and the other was $4000. She said I could look at some places in nearby Palms or Mar Vista that might be cheaper. I don't mean to cast aspersion on anyone who lives in Palms or Mar Vista, but I had lived all my life in zip code 90402 and I could feel my heart starting to race at the thought of having to move any place else. The $3750 apartment was on Wilshire Boulevard near Santa Monica Hospital and I know that ambulances go down Wilshire at all hours with their sirens blaring. The $4000 apartment was on Chelsea Street, a few blocks south of Wilshire, about ten blocks from our house on Marguerita. I totaled all of my expenses and made a monthly budget including food, gasoline, car insurance, internet and cable TV, books and videogames, subscription to my aviation magazines, clothing, movie tickets, telephone, dog food for Sadie and membership in the Santa Monica YMCA. The total was $2,600 a month. That would leave me $400 a month left over from my $7000 for emergencies. I am concerned that I will be handicapped in reaching my goal of having over 3000 Yelp reviews if I am short of money for going to restaurants. Amy told me there were other people waiting to see the apartment on Chelsea and that if I couldn't put down a deposit quickly I might lose it. The apartment was on the top floor and Amy told me that would mean that I wouldn't have to hear footsteps from other tenants over my head. I never even considered footsteps on the ceiling, but I know I wouldn't like that. Amy said I would have to pay first and last month's rent plus a security deposit, which came to $10,100. I had more than that saved in my regular Wells Fargo bank account, so I was able to write a check and I signed the lease for one year. Amy thanked me and she also gave me a very nice carabiner keychain that has the name and number for West LA Rentals stamped on the side.

Treasure Trove Estate Sales ★★

One of the things that happens after your house gets sold is that you have to take everything out of it. In my mother's house, that means acres of stuff. The house is 4,212 square feet with four bedrooms and five bathrooms and it was just full of furniture, paintings and clothes and books. After the house was sold, my sister, Lisa, hired Treasure Trove Estate Sales to sell all of the furniture and clothes and things that were left over after she took what she wanted. My stepfather, Carl, is moving back onto his Catalina 36 sailboat in the Marina which is where he stayed before he met Mother, so all he had room for were some pictures of him and my mom, some with me in them, a Bose radio from the kitchen and an old brass telescope that we had in the living room. Carl told me that I should not be shy and make sure I take anything I want, but there isn't much room in my new apartment now that I have moved things from my old place over the garage. I asked Lisa if I could take the Osterizer from the kitchen because sometimes I like to make banana and date milkshakes. She said okay. I also asked her if I could have our grandfather's old Rolex chronometer watch which Mother kept in a drawer because it reminded her of him. Mother had shown it to me, but didn't want me to wear it because it was valuable and she was afraid I would lose it or a robber might take it away. When I asked Lisa about it she said, that Mother had already promised that watch to her son, Adam, and if I had wanted it I should have let Mother know before and now Adam was counting on it. I wish I had asked Mother. Lisa said she would buy me a new Casio if I like so I asked for the model SGW300 which has an altimeter built in as well as a thermometer and five alarms. I am not exactly sure about all of the things Lisa kept for herself and her family, but I know she took most of Mother's jewelry and a few paintings and some silverware. Lisa said they were things that wouldn't interest me and I guess she is right. I also asked about Mother's BMW 528i which would be a step up from my 1984 Mercedes that I call Atomic Betty and that I still like very much, but Lisa said the BMW was leased and would have to go back to the leasing company. Nobody from the family was allowed to be at the estate sale. Not even Lisa. Mr. Haddad, who owns Treasure Trove Estate Sales says buyers are uncomfortable if a member of the family is watching. That was fine with me, because I didn't want to be around when people drive off with things that belonged to Mother. I was in my new apartment playing *Legend of Grimrock* on my computer when suddenly I realized something very upsetting. Although I had moved out of my childhood bedroom in the house and into the garage apartment six years ago and Mother had turned the bedroom into a room for doing her art, I may have left some things behind in the closet, just some old clothes and some school books and things like that. But suddenly, I remembered that I had left my Star Wars Tusken Raiders Sandpeople 1/6 scale collectible figure in the closet. That's why I kept it in the closet, so the box wouldn't fade from sunlight. I bought it at the 2013 Star Wars Celebration at the Anaheim Convention Center and it was new and never opened. Tusken Raiders sold out long ago, so it is very hard to find, especially in original wrapping. It cost me $200 then but I saw that Dreamworld Comics in Mar Vista had one on the shelf with a faded box for $800. I didn't know how to reach Mr. Haddad and I called Lisa, but she said that it was too late and that I shouldn't go over there and that she didn't have his telephone number. If somebody at the sale knew anything at all about Stars Wars Figures they would snap it up so I got in my car and got there as quick as I could. There were lots of customers walking in and out and there was a table with a cashbox that had been set up on the front walk. Mr. Haddad was inside the front door and I asked him if he had sold my Tusken Raider. He reminded me that family had agreed not to come to the sale, but I said I just wanted to get my Tusken Raider and would leave. He asked the man at the cash box if it had been sold and (oh no!) the man said it was one of the first things to go. I asked how much he sold it for and he said he thought it was $10. I asked if he could tell me who bought it, because I would try to get it back, but he said all sales are final. I told him that he shouldn't have sold it, especially for $10. Then their uniformed security guard came over and asked if he could walk me to my car. I told him that I just wanted to get back my Tusken Raider, but he wouldn't listen and told me that I would have to leave. I was very upset and I went out to the sidewalk and I was walking back and forth, trying to decide what to do. Mr. Haddad asked if he should call my sister. I told him no and I left. Considering how much money Treasure Trove must have made in commission on the sale you would think they would be able to be more helpful. Also, if they are in the business of conducting estate sales and evaluating things, they should certainly know the value of a NIB (new in box) Sideshow Collectible Tusken Raider Sandpeople figurine and not sell it for $10. I am so angry I would like to give them one star but that would leave me nowhere to go if I have another review for someone who is worse.

The Misunderstood Restaurant and Bar ★ ★ ★

Where is Mr. Understood?! My sister, Lisa, called to say that she wanted to come over and see my apartment and take me out for a bite to eat. Lisa is up on the trendy restaurants and I always could use a new place to review for Yelp. She said she had to drop my nephew, Adam, off for a tennis lesson at Reed Park in Santa Monica and she would have 45 minutes to spend. This was the first time she has come to my apartment so I made sure it was clean and that there weren't any smelly clothes in the hamper. I think she really liked the apartment, because she inspected all around and looked out the front window and told me what a great view I had. She asked me how much I was paying and when I told her she asked if I could afford that much. I said that it was important to me to live in the old neighborhood and also to be able to keep Sadie and that I had cut down on other things. She asked me how long my lease was for and if I needed to give the landlord a pet deposit, but I didn't know what that was and she said it was an extra deposit in case your dog does damage. Sadie has very good manners and wouldn't need a deposit, but in any case I don't think I paid one. My lease is for a year. She told me she was just asking because I had to be careful with my money or it wouldn't last forever and I said that I was being careful. We didn't have much time left after Lisa saw my apartment but we did go to The Misunderstood Restaurant and Grille. I wanted to take Sadie and sit on their patio which I think allows dogs, but Lisa said she wanted to sit inside. It is a very good looking room with a long bar with dark wood tones. I know that most of their customers are millennials, which I am as well because technically I am someone who reached young adulthood in the twenty-first century. I had the ahi tuna burger and Lisa got the Tuscan kale-quinoa salad. The tuna burger was delicious, but when I asked for some mayonnaise on the side, the waitress forgot it. Lisa ate half her salad although she said it was very good. I like salads that come in big bowls, but this came on a small plate. I know kale and quinoa is supposed to be very good for you and they have roughage and antioxidants, but kale tastes too much like grass. I do like quinoa, though. I read that poor villagers in the mountains of Ecuador who are used to regularly having quinoa in their diet can't afford it anymore because Americans have driven up the price so much. I didn't mention that to Lisa as she seemed to be enjoying her salad and probably wouldn't like to have heard about the Ecuadorians. I would like to go to Ecuador someday. If so I would choose Avianca Airlines which flies Airbus A320s, a very safe airplane with a crash rating of 0.10 per million departures, second only to the Boeing 737 at 0.08 (not the 737 MAX which is a very different plane). The bill was fifty-four dollars with two fancy sodas and I thought that was too expensive for what we had, but Lisa paid in a hurry because she had to pick up Adam and she asked me if I minded walking back home which I didn't mind because I could walk in the park to get back to my apartment and I like that. I am only giving Misunderstood three stars because the server was not very attentive and the food which wasn't bad seemed too expensive for what it was. I won't blame Misunderstood Bar and Grille for what is happening to the Ecuadorians.

Otto's German Auto Repair of Santa Monica ★ ★ ★ ★

I was on Wilshire Boulevard on my way to the Santa Monica YMCA on 5th Street for my Tuesday Zumba exercise class while driving Atomic Betty, my trusty old Mercedes 300 sedan, when I heard this big metal-hitting-metal banging and crunching noise come out of the front and then Betty just stopped dead in the middle of traffic. People started beeping their horns for me to move, but the engine wouldn't start and then two men from a pickup truck behind me pushed me off to a parking space while I steered. I called the AAA and the tow truck driver suggested he tow Atomic Betty to Otto's which was nearby on Santa Monica Boulevard that he said works on German cars. At the repair shop the service manager, Yuri, told me that the timing chain had broken which made the valves crash into the pistons and destroy the engine. He asked me if I ever checked the timing chain and I told him I didn't know what the timing chain was. He said it would cost me $8000 to rebuild the engine and that a 1984 Mercedes 300D was worth only about $3000 when running. I am attached to Atomic Betty and I was thinking maybe I would just pay to replace her engine, but he told me I should get a smaller, more economical car and suggested a Honda Civic. I do know Hondas are supposed to be very reliable. I asked him how much a new Civic would cost and he said about $24,000 with taxes. I told him I couldn't pay that much and I really didn't want to ask Ms. Reese, my estate trustee for money so soon after we started our arrangement. Yuri then told me that I could see his friend, Sergei, who owns a used car lot two blocks down the street. He called up Sergei who said he had two used Honda Civics and could give me a very good deal because I was a friend of Yuri so I went over there. Four stars and thanks to Yuri who couldn't fix my car but tried to help.

Classy Classics of Santa Monica ★ ★ ★ ★

When I walked onto the car lot Sergei was already expecting me because Yuri, the mechanic who recommended him, had called before. He asked if I liked a blue car or a gray car because he had both. My recently deceased 1984 Mercedes 300D, Atomic Betty, is blue and I like blue. He said that the blue car was a 2011 and it only had 42,000 miles and looked and drove like it was new. It was in a back corner of the lot and it was all clean and waxed with that shiny polish on the tires. It was much cleaner than Atomic Betty ever was, even after I had taken her to the car wash (note to self to review Bright Star Car Wash). There was a price sign on the windshield that said $13,999. After having just paid the deposit and rent for my apartment that was more money than I had in the bank. He said that 2011 was the best year for Civics because the newer models are full of complicated electronics that are always breaking and that I would be better off with a 2011 model that has good safety features but is simple to operate. I sat in it and it smelled like air freshener inside, but the dashboard and other parts were all shined up and there were even paper mats on the floor to keep it clean. He asked if I was ready to buy a car today because if so he could give me a special deal. I wouldn't be there if I didn't need a car right away but I told him I didn't have $13,999 in my bank account. He explained that wouldn't be a problem and that only millionaires buy a car with all cash and I should pay for it with monthly payments. Atomic Betty was Grandma Rose's old car that I inherited when she stopped driving, so I never really bought a car on my own. He asked if I had good credit. I already knew from getting my new apartment that I had a credit score of 782 which Amy Rosenberg, my realtor, said was very good and was probably because I had two credit cards in my name that my mother had taken out for me years ago. Sergei asked me how much I could pay a month and I said I didn't want to pay anything a month which was true but Sergei laughed. He said he could get me payments of $385 a month if I put $1000 down. I had enough in my bank account for that, but if I paid for my apartment and $385 a month for a car I wouldn't have money for food. I didn't know what to do so I excused myself and I called Emma. This time she came right on the phone and I told her my problem and she asked me if it was a good car and I said I thought so and she said that I needed a car in Los Angeles and not to worry about it and that I could buy it and that Mother's estate would help. I wanted to ask her more, but she said she was busy and had to get off the phone. This put me somewhat at ease, but getting a new apartment and a new car, not to mention a new dog made me really, really nervous. I guess Sergei could tell that and he asked me what was worrying me and I told him. We went into Sergei's office and he filled out the paperwork for me. The price was $13,995 as he said, but there was tax of about $1200 and some extras that I needed to pay for—license and documentation fees and then Sergei said that I should get the upholstery treated with Scotchguard because I have a dog, and also I should purchase ceramic coating as I don't have an enclosed garage, and also I should get an extended warranty because I have already learned the lesson of not having a car warranty. This all came to a lot more than $13,995. The payment was no longer $385, but $447. I told Sergei that I needed to make sure that was okay with Emma, but she was in a business meeting when I called. Sergei asked me if I was serious about buying because he had another customer who would like to buy this car. I think he may have been disappointed with me for not being able to say yes right away. Anyway I said yes and signed the papers and then he gave me the keys to my new car. I drove it straight back to the apartment because I had left Sadie in her crate several hours ago and I know she definitely needed a walk. The Honda drove very smooth and the seats were comfortable. Even if it sounds like I am being unfaithful to Atomic Betty it is also nice that the glove box door doesn't rattle like before. Afterwards Emma Reese called me back from the bank and I told her about buying the Honda. She asked me a few questions about the contract and asked me to send it to her. Although I had spent much less than a new car Emma didn't seem as pleased as me, but she said she would take care of everything and make sure the car payment was made. She also suggested I not enter into any new contracts without consulting her and I said I wouldn't.

Jiffy Juice ★ ★ ★ ★ ★

I plan to keep going up Pico Boulevard for restaurants, but this review is about Jiffy Juice on Santa Monica Boulevard near the library where I work. I always walk over there on Wednesday in the afternoon after my 12–4 shift in the library. I always order the same, a Peach Plantation smoothie, medium size and I get a straw but no lid. This time I had to wait to order because there was a girl, about sixteen or seventeen years old, in front of me and she ordered a Protein Berry smoothie with a zinc and vitamin boost. She was wearing jeans that have big holes in them on purpose and she was texting while she ordered, which I think is very rude. The server was new for the Wednesday afternoon shift and her name tag said "Alison P." She was Asian—I can't tell if maybe Japanese or Chinese, with black hair in a ponytail and I thought she was really cute. She wore two little earrings on her right ear only. After Alison put the ingredients in the mixer and started mixing, the young woman customer suddenly put her phone away and said "Sorry, I have to go," and she just walked out the door without even paying. Alison P. started to say something to her, but the girl was already gone. Alison kind of rolled her eyes at me. She said she'd be right with me and she finished mixing the shake and then she asked me if I'd like a free Protein Berry smoothie. I told her I always get peach, but she smiled and said if I didn't want it she would have to throw it out. I said yes, part because I could save eight dollars, but part because she was being so nice I didn't want to say no to her. After a few minutes Alison asked me if I like the berry as much as the peach. I couldn't lie and said I would order the peach next time, but Protein Berry, which is made with strawberries and bananas and soy milk, tasted pretty good although I don't think the zinc and vitamin boosters helped the flavor. There weren't any other customers around and she asked me if I lived nearby and I told her that I lived on Marguerita Street. She said that I lived in a very nice area and she shared a little apartment in Westwood because she is going to UCLA and studying psychology. I made a kind of a joke and said maybe she'd like to study me and she said she bet it would be interesting, whatever that meant. Before I left I put three dollars in the tip jar for her. Next time I will still order

Peach Plantation. I am rating Jiffy Juice Brentwood five stars, but that is generous as I am really giving the five stars to Alison P. who I think is really cute and nice.

Jiffy Juice Brentwood (Additional Review) ★ ★

I went to Jiffy Juice again today for my Wednesday Peach Plantation smoothie. I hoped that I might find Alison P., their best server ever, although I didn't expect to be so lucky as to get a free smoothie like last time. Alison was behind the counter but when I walked in, I said hello and made an effort to look at her in the eyes, instead of at my shoes, which is something that Dr. DeSantis has encouraged me to do. I know that if I ever expect to get a great wife that I am going to have to get good at looking at people and also at both asking questions and listening. What was strange was that when I looked at Alison she didn't really look back. I would say she looked everywhere but at me. I asked her for a medium Peach Passion and she nodded and turned away to begin making it. She kept her back to me which was kind of disappointing. Meanwhile I was trying to figure out something cool to say. I was thinking about asking her what her major was, but she told me before it was psychology. And if I asked her about UCLA then what if she asked me about where I went to school and I would have to say that I just went to Santa Monica Community College for two semesters and then dropped out? When she finished the shake and did turn around she said kind of a frosty way, "That will be $7.99 — You know you got me in trouble with my boss." She handed me the cup and I put my credit card in the machine. "I don't know why you had to put it up in Yelp that I gave you a free smoothie. My boss saw that and I nearly got fired." I told her I was sorry and that I didn't mean to get her in trouble, but then another customer came in and she had to take care of them, so I feel like I didn't really get a chance to explain. I am not at all mad at Alison who is a very good person, but I am mad at her boss. I do understand that by her giving me a smoothie for free it meant that I didn't buy one for myself that time but it is not right to just throw a good smoothie away. Also, I think it is shortsighted of her boss not to realize that customer loyalty is important and Alison's variety of thoughtfulness would make me a customer for life. The two stars are for Alison's boss, not for Alison who is five stars. If you see him you could tell him to be nicer to his employees.

Jiffy Juice (2ND Additional Review) ★ ★ ★

This update to my last review really isn't for Jiffy Juice. It is just to set the record straight. I don't think I reacted the right way when Alison told me the other day that I got her in trouble with her boss. When I had time to think about it I realized that I must have put her in a very bad position and I should have taken responsibility for that. I think that she gave me the smoothie partly because it was an extra smoothie and she didn't feel right just dumping it into the sink, but also I don't think she would have given it to just anyone. I mean if it was some creepy, weird old guy that was spitting and swearing, she probably wouldn't have given it to him. I am using an extreme example to make a point. These sorts of calculations are the hardest ones for me to make. Dr. DeSantis sometimes helps me think them out, but I think it is totally possible Alison may have actually been attracted to me. Maybe it was because she could tell I was attracted to her. They call that mutual attraction. I know she caught me looking at her and she looked back and smiled a kind of personal smile. I didn't want to go back to Jiffy Juice in Brentwood since "the incident," because I didn't want to make any more trouble for Alison. I thought about it a lot and I decided I wanted her to know how sorry I was so I bought a dozen really nice yellow roses at Barrington Farm and went over to the store at 7 p.m. when they close. The woman at the flower department suggested tulips, but I thought roses would be better when I told her that it was to apologize for a mistake that I made with a special person and she agreed. I waited on the curb for Alison to come out and I stood up when I saw her come out the door. She was wearing jeans and a nice blue blouse and she had on a red backpack. I guess she didn't expect to see me and asked what I was doing. I told her that I wanted to say I was sorry and then I handed her the roses. At first she said she didn't want them, but then she took them. She didn't thank me right away, but when I asked her if things were going better at work now, she said that they were and then she thanked me for the roses and said she had to get home to study for exams. I asked her what classes she was taking, but she said she saw her bus coming across the street and she had to go. She ran across the street on a red light which I would never do at that busy intersection but she made it okay and got on the bus. I was glad she took the flowers and I don't know if I will see her again, but at least I tried to make things right. And I really don't have any bad feelings for Jiffy Juice.

West Marine ★ ★ ★ ★ ★

Carl, my stepfather, said that he would take me out sailing on his boat Saturday morning. He has a Catalina 36 boat which (in case you didn't guess) is 36 feet long. It is named "Guillaumet" after a very tall mountain that he once climbed in Patagonia, Chile. Carl met my mother when she was on a hiking trip in Bhutan and Carl was working there as a guide. In addition to being a sailor and a musician, Carl is a mountain climber although he does it less these days since he grew older (he is 58 years old) and also since, according to Carl, mountain climbing became "too much of a business." Carl returned to staying on Guillaumet after we moved out of the house on Marguerita Street. He said that he likes it because the small space keeps him from accumulating too much "stuff." Carl needed a part for the boat, a "line jammer" to keep one of the ropes that goes up the mast from slipping, so before sailing we went to West Marine. Carl says that, on sailboats, you always say "line" and not "rope" except for the rope that ties the boat to the dock. Also Carl asked the salesman to show him a Raymarine Automagic autopilot for his boat. Carl said the Raymarine was one of the best and it would be a good thing to have when he sailed solo to Santa Cruz Island but that he would have to put off buying it because it was too expensive. At the checkout Carl had me try on a cap that said "Born Sailor" on it and then he bought it for me. After he got the line jammer installed I helped him pull on the halyard to raise the mainsail and we went for a sail around the harbor and then around the breakwater. Carl said he was playing fiddle on the bandstand in the park with some musician friends later and I could come watch him if I liked. He let me steer most of the time until we came back to the dock and then he steered us into the slip. West Marine seems to have everything one could possibly need for a boat and the store is very clean and well organized.

Number One Doughnuts ★ ★ ★ ★ ★

The best thing about Number One Doughnuts is the "Marcus Katz" doughnut. Yes, it really is named after me. That is because I have been going there for doughnuts since I was a little boy and the owners know me. Number One Doughnuts has been there for sixty years which is thirty-eight years before I was born and ten years before Mother was born. My dad, Stephen Katz, used to take me there sometimes when I was very little, about five. My favorite doughnut back then was a chocolate doughnut with sprinkles. I am not talking about chocolate glaze. I mean a chocolate cake doughnut with a sugar glaze and sprinkles on it. My dad had three cars of his own, but I always wanted him to take me in his Morgan Plus Four convertible. It was thirty years old even back then, but he had it all restored like new. After he and Mother got divorced when I was three he would come on some Saturdays and pick me up and we might go to the park or to the beach, but he would always bring his Morgan because I liked the rumble of the exhaust and the wind in my face. Once we went to a drive-in movie in it and saw "A Bug's Life." I hate the thought of the Morgan now, because that is the car that got in the terrible accident that killed him. A Morgan's frame is made partly out of wood and doesn't hold up in a crash. Because I insisted, Mother would sometimes take me to Number One Doughnuts after Dad's accident and I think that the owner was especially nice to me because he knew my dad had died and partly because I am a little different from most of the kids he sees every day. Believe it or not, some people get kind of bored with "neurotypical" kids and like the change of pace that somebody like me offers. When I was nine my mother took me to Number One and Sam, the owner, asked me if I wanted to create a special doughnut and he would name it after me. I thought that was a great idea and I said I would like a plain cake doughnut with maple frosting, bacon bits and blueberries. He took me in the back of the store and I helped him make three custom doughnuts, one for him, one for Mother and one for me. Everybody agreed that it was delicious and so the Marcus Doughnut was born. I would like to give Number One Doughnuts six stars if I could.

Aaahs Gifts and Cards ★ ★ ★ ★ ★

Thursday was Carl's fifty-ninth birthday. I went to Rite Aid to look for a card for him, but they didn't have anything that I thought he would like, so I went to Aaahs on Wilshire Boulevard where they have thousands of cards in a big room on the second floor. They really have a great selection. I even found three cards that were just for step-dads. One was for a step-dad who likes golf, but Carl doesn't play golf. Another was kind of mean. It said "Happy Birthday from the Kid You Inherited When You Shacked up with My Mom." I chose the one that said "I'm glad you <u>stepped</u> into my life." And inside it says "Happy Birthday to a great step-dad." Now that I have money I thought I should buy him a nice present. Last year I bought him a sweater, but my mother was the one who picked it out and she paid for it, too. The only thing I could think of that he really wanted was an autopilot for his boat that we saw at West Marine, but that is $3000 and after I paid for my apartment and everything for Sadie I don't have enough left. I'll try to think of something else.

West Marine (Update) ★ ★ ★ ★ ★

My step-dad, Carl, really wants a Raymarine autopilot for his sailboat so he can sail single handedly to Santa Cruz Island where he sometimes likes to camp out. He used to try to get my mother to go with him, but she never really liked camping although she did enjoy sailing on his boat. The only problem was that the Raymarine EV200 autopilot was $3295 and although I guess I have plenty of money since Mother died, I have a budget that I need to keep to. But also Carl has been nicer to me than anyone I know of except my mother. Carl is very handy. He put in my new kitchen cabinets and sink in my old apartment behind the house and together we built a 1/100th flyable model of a Douglas A-1 Skyraider. We took it to Hansen Dam recreation area and flew it there. Carl was the one who first found Dr. DeSantis for me which was a big improvement over the psychiatrist that I was seeing at CAN (the UCLA <u>C</u>hild and Adult <u>N</u>eurodevelopment <u>Clin</u>ic) and I am so much better now because of it. When I went into West Marine just to look for some kind of sailboat gift I was surprised to see that the autopilot was on sale at 15% off, a big saving, but still really expensive. The salesman said I could put it on my credit card and pay it off monthly. I had never done that, but had always automatically paid off the balance on my credit card when the bill came due. That is how Mother showed me to do it. He asked if I had enough credit on it and I know that I have $12,000 less the hundred dollars or so I have used this month. I asked him how much I would have to pay monthly and he didn't know, but he suggested I call Wells Fargo Visa whose 800 number was right on the card and the representative told me that it would add about $120 a month to my card. I could afford an extra $120 a month since Emma Reese told me she would help with my car payments, so I told the salesman I would buy it. Also he said that if Carl has any trouble installing it that he could come back to the store and they would help him. West Marine didn't giftwrap, but I took it to the card store a few doors down and they found some navy blue paper that seemed nautical. When I gave the present to Carl at his boat he was surprised to see a present and acted all excited when he unwrapped it but then he looked serious kind of unhappy or disappointed and said that it was too big a present and he couldn't accept it. I told him that I had calculated I could afford it on my budget and that he would hurt my feelings if he didn't take it. He insisted I return it, but I told him I wouldn't and held my ground. We finally agreed that he would hold on to it for a little while (there is a thirty day return policy) and we would decide later. I think he will decide that he wants it. I hope so.

A Message from Durinda Dowling

I have been getting many messages through Yelp from my readers and followers. I have been tempted to include some of them, mostly because they are nice and complimentary. A few of them have been sort of mean but I try not to let those ones upset me and if they seem like they are going to be mean I try not to read all the way through. But nice or nasty, they are private messages and I don't think it is right to publish them and it may even not be legal. There are a few messages from just one person that I did think I would like to include here, even if it means breaking the format of my book and Heather, my editor agrees. I asked Durinda Dowling for permission to reprint her messages and I am including them here.

Dear Marcus,

My name is Durinda Dowling and I live in Creswell, Oregon, a small town just outside of Eugene. I am writing to tell you that I have read all of your reviews and I check in every day to see if there are new ones posted. I have been diagnosed as being somewhat on the spectrum myself with an AQ score of 34. I think your idea of choosing a street (Pico Boulevard) and reviewing every restaurant on it is absolutely brilliant. When I saw it I wished I had thought to do the same thing and I bet other Yelpers will copy you with your very cool idea. I know that you said to some people this kind of attention to detail may show signs of OCD but I can tell from your writing that you are a very introspective and aware person so I hope you are comfortable with your operating system. When you mentioned how much you respected Harrison Ford I wanted to remind you that Harrison Ford has OCD, as did Einstein and Marcel Proust and Stanley Kubrick. What I like most about your reviews is that you seem like a very real and honest person and I think you are very brave to talk about yourself the way you do. I am also a reviewer on Yelp and, in fact, I have been a Yelp Elite for two years and have posted 1237 reviews. Perhaps you will read some of them, although they are almost all about Eugene (a great place to live) and Portland where I sometimes visit but I haven't ever dared to be as revealing as you. Although I am on the spectrum, I am lucky I have managed to get a degree in biochemistry and I maintain a job in the lab at the University of Oregon in Eugene for twenty hours a week and am fortunate to be able to say that my parents are alive and together and that I have a very good group situation on a small farm community where we grow produce here in Creswell. There are very few dumb rules but all the residents are really nice and everyone gets along well most of the time. I am so sorry that your experience was so bad. It was hard for me to leave home at first, and life is not a bed of roses, but now I know that being in the right community has been a good thing for me.

Law Firm of Shapiro, Sussman and Gross ★ ★ ★ ★ ★

This is very, very upsetting to write about but I think people out there need to hear about what has happened to me. I received a registered letter two days ago. The mail woman rang my bell and then I had to sign for it. It came from the Superior Court of Los Angeles Probate Division. Inside there was a notice to appear before the court the next month because my sister, Lisa, had filed a petition to the court to get conservatorship of me because I am on the spectrum. I have heard of conservatorships but they should be for people who are much more severely affected than me and have difficulty taking care of themselves. I am very surprised that Lisa didn't even talk to me about her plan before she went to the court. Surprised isn't even the word. I am shocked. Worse than shocked. The first thing I did was to call my stepfather, Carl. When I told him, he was very angry. He said he suspected it might be because Lisa wanted to get at my inheritance. Because Lisa and her husband both have good jobs and she received quite a lot from my mother I found that hard to believe. I would rather think that although she is misguided, she has my best interests at heart. In any case, Carl made an appointment for us to see Barbara Sussman who is an attorney that he knows through his boating community and she specializes in this sort of law. The office in downtown Santa Monica is very pleasant and the receptionist offered us water and had Hershey's kisses on the counter of which I took several. Carl and Barbara talked about boats for a few minutes before we got down to business. I showed the letter to Barbara and then Carl and I explained that before my mother died she set up a trust that gave fifty percent to me and thirty percent to Lisa. Carl said that he thought Lisa was resentful that she didn't share equally but that is really wrong-headed. Because the trust passes on to Lisa and her children if something happens to me, Barbara said it would be in her interest to keep me from spending it down. When Carl asked Barbara if she could represent me in court and explain to the judge what is going on, Barbara said that only the probate court can appoint an attorney for the respondent (that's me) and that she wouldn't be allowed to represent me. Carl wanted to know if the attorney would be able to stop Lisa and she said that it depended on the attorney that the judge chose. She said that the judge in my court, Judge Albert Hughes, was known to choose attorneys who took the side of the conservators. I asked if there was anything we could do. Barbara said that the only strategy she could suggest was for Carl to also file for conservatorship if that was okay by me. Even though Carl would then be my conservator, he would probably act more in my interest and wouldn't try to boss me around or tell me how to spend the money that Mother gave to me. Carl seemed surprised by the suggestion and we both said we needed to think about that. Barbara seemed to know a lot about the law and about probate court which she explained works differently from the regular courts. She explained that the official reason the judge picks the lawyer from a list he keeps to represent me is that some people who are mentally disabled might be influenced by a relative or someone else to pick an attorney who wouldn't act in their best interests. What doesn't make sense is that I am the person who will have to pay the fees for this attorney from my estate. This is not a good system. It's too bad that Barbara is not allowed to represent me because I feel she would always act in my best interests.

Another Message from Durinda

This is a new message from Durinda and I think it's a good idea to include this one. You'll see why later.

Hello Marcus. Congratulations or reaching 237 reviews in

such a short time. I check every morning for new ones and I was very upset when I saw the review of the law firm, Shapiro, Sussman and Gross. I think you are very brave to share this, but it makes me worry about you. There are a few people in my community who are under conservatorships and some of the conservators are good and some are bad. I know there are organizations that are set up to help with conservatorship problems and I could find out about them if you like. The big news I am writing to tell you is that there is a Yelp Elite Western Regional event that is scheduled to take place in Los Angeles in three weeks. Normally I only go to the events that are close to me in Oregon. Yelpers meet fellow yelpers at these events and they are always sponsored by different restaurants and food companies that want Elites to write about them to drum up business. Even though the rules say you aren't allowed to write about the event itself, you can write about your experience if you go to their restaurant later. I try to be very honorable and not let the event color my review, but I don't mind eating their food ☺. BTW I do love to eat and I am kind of curvy, but I am not really fat I don't think. Just saying ☺. Anyway I was thinking that maybe I could go to the LA event (I think it is at a hotel somewhere near the airport) and then maybe we could meet. I could probably get you in as a guest to one of the food tastings and also maybe we could go to a restaurant and each review it. Maybe we could go together to your next stop on Pico Blvd. Wouldn't that be cool?

This is very exciting news for me and I hope that Durinda does decide to come down. I wrote back to tell her just that.

Frank Tuttle, Attorney ★

Because my sister, Lisa, has filed for conservatorship of me, Judge Hughes in Los Angeles Superior Court Probate Division has appointed Mr. Frank Tuttle as my attorney. He is one on the list of attorneys that the judge can appoint and he is supposed to represent me in probate court. I say "supposed" because I don't think he is doing a very good job. While I do face challenges that neurotypicals don't face, I function pretty well and don't believe that I need anyone standing over me every second to run my life. And if I were to choose someone it definitely wouldn't be my sister, Lisa. Frank had a copy of the legal request for conservatorship and he asked me a bunch of questions about how much Mother had helped me with finances and things before she died and how much I had depended on her and also how much I had been spending since. I could see where he was going, but that was because Mother had played a big part in my life from the beginning and that didn't mean I needed a replacement to do all of those things. I am older and more responsible now, even if I am not perfect. He said that he thought the strain of having to maintain an apartment and a car was probably a big challenge for me and why didn't I just relax about those things and think more about my peace of mind and well-being? He said he thought I was lucky that I had a family member who was willing to step up for me. He also suggested that I give a group home another try. I tried to explain to him that what would make me the happiest is to be independent and to run my own life. Also to find a girlfriend and wife, but I didn't think he or the court could do anything about that. I asked him if Lisa was my conservator if she could have any say in who my friends are or who I might want to get married to if I ever wanted to. He asked if I had a girl in mind and I said no, but that didn't mean that it won't happen and I wouldn't want to have to ask Lisa's permission if I did. What I don't understand is that if he is my lawyer why isn't he working to support what I am asking him to do? He said that he has a responsibility to me, but he also has a responsibility to the court. That doesn't make any sense to me. He is <u>my</u> lawyer. In fact the court requires that I pay him myself. Just meeting with him to tell me these things cost my estate $700! And this is all because they are supposedly concerned that I am not handling my money properly! I don't want him to do anything illegal or unethical. I just want him to be my advocate. If I were accused of murder I wouldn't expect my attorney to side with the prosecutor even if I actually had murdered someone. That's how the American legal system is supposed to work.

Law Offices of Eleanor Sanchez ★ ★ ★ ★ ★

I am in a really difficult position because my sister, Lisa, has applied to the court for conservatorship of me after my mother died as I am on the autism spectrum. My court-appointed lawyer, Frank Tuttle, won't properly defend me against Lisa. Another lawyer, (I can't believe how my life has suddenly become crowded with lawyers) Barbara Sussman, suggested that my stepfather, Carl, whom I trust, should apply for a conservatorship and the court might grant my request to choose him. She said that she wasn't able to handle this case, but she recommended Eleanor Sanchez. Carl and I went to Eleanor's office which is in an office building in Marina del Rey. Carl did most of the explaining and Eleanor seemed to understand the problem right away. She asked me questions about my mother and Lisa and Carl and made sure that I understood that Carl would wind up with a lot of power over my life. Even though he didn't say so, I don't think Carl really liked the idea. He wanted to know what his responsibilities would be. He said that he had gotten an offer to tour with a good band and he was looking forward to traveling and playing music. This was the first I had heard about it. Eleanor said that Northwestern Trust could continue financial oversight and he could delegate any other responsibilities. I told her that the best thing was to have no conservator, but if there has to be one then I trust Carl and not Lisa. Eleanor explained that although the court was supposed to have my best interests at heart, it didn't always work out that way. She said that she was not a fan of Judge

Hughes and that she had some experience with my court-appointed attorney, Frank Tuttle. I could see she really didn't want to say anything bad about another attorney, but she did say that his getting on the judge's list of probate attorneys was all about court politics. She said she would prepare the petition for Carl to be my conservator and that there would be a hearing in front of Judge Hughes. The judge would probably want to ask me some questions and it would be important for me to be calm and make it clear what my wishes are.

Rock & Roll Ale House El Segundo ★ ★

Meet here and eat someplace else! The big news is that Durinda, my friend on Yelp from Eugene, Oregon, came to Los Angeles. She messaged and invited me to meet her at an actual Elite event at Rock & Roll Ale House in El Segundo near the Los Angeles Airport. I was really excited about meeting Durinda and about going to an Elite event where all the restaurants give out free food. When I got there she was waiting in front. I recognized her from her Yelp picture, except that her hair had a big pink streak and she was wearing pink eyeglasses. She was definitely curvy like she had already told me, but she didn't seem overly fat. She waved when she recognized me. Then we said hello and she told me how glad she was to meet me in person. Durinda said she was sorry but the event was being held in a separate party room and she just found out that they weren't allowed to bring guests, but if I could wait she would sneak some food out to me, probably ribs and chicken wings. Television screens showed sports on every wall in the main room and they were blaring really dumb pop music through speakers in the ceiling. It was a couple of minutes before Durinda came back out with a napkin that had a gray-looking hamburger slider and some soggy fried zucchini. But the great and amazing thing is that some other Yelp Elites came out with her just to meet me. Fortunately they were all wearing name tags. Jenny, Sean, Nguyen, Richard, Jose,

Farhad, Myrna and a few whose names I already forgot. I don't know what I expected, but they definitely weren't hipsters, except maybe Jose, who was wearing a short jacket with sequins sewed on it and a bow tie. He talked a lot and was very funny. I think that Sean may have been on the spectrum because he was always looking down when he talked. I'd say I had a mixed feeling of relief and disappointment to see that Elites were not royalty, but regular, nice people. Farhad said that he had read every one of my reviews and thought they were really great and insightful. That made me feel good. Durinda said she was sorry I couldn't go in with her, but I wasn't missing much. I think neither of us liked this Rock & Roll Ale House which is too bad, but it was nice that we agree about things right off the bat. She asked me if there was someplace else we could go. She suggested we go to my next scheduled stop on Pico Boulevard together.

Samo Pizza Pico Boulevard Stop #13 ★ ★ ★ ★
(Note to book readers: Pico Boulevard stops 5–12: El Texate, Boba Lab, Firehouse Subs, Yogurtland, El Pollo Loco, Pita House, Buffalo's World Famous Wings, Fatburger have been left out of the book. I couldn't possibly include all of my reviews and these reviews weren't very interesting anyway because they are mini-mall style chains except for El Texate which got four stars.)

Where the Elite meet! The BIG NEWS, is that my friend Durinda who is visiting from Eugene, Oregon, and is a genuine Yelp Elite said she wanted to come along to my next scheduled stop on my Pico Boulevard dining odyssey, traveling east from the beach and eating at every restaurant. I wish I was scheduled for someplace really special for Durinda, but she insisted that we go to my planned next stop which was SaMo Pizza. SaMo Pizza already has a 4 and a half star Yelp rating, so I expected the pizza would be pretty good, but otherwise it is a standard pizza restaurant in a mini-mall across the street from Santa

Monica College where you order at the counter. On the plus side I haven't had a chance to review a pizza restaurant yet and I love pizza, but not quite as much as fish tacos. I think the oven is probably the most important ingredient in making pizza. Wood-fired brick ovens are definitely best, but a big cast iron pizza oven is not a deal breaker. I tried to be a good host and asked Durinda what pizza she would like from the menu and she said I was the expert and should decide. I asked her if she liked the Capricciosa which is mozzarella, ham, mushrooms, Kalamata olives, oregano with Marinara sauce and she said that sounded great. She offered to pay for half, but I didn't think that was fair as she had brought me out some food from Rock & Roll Ale House Stop earlier, even though it wasn't that good. We also ordered a Mediterranean salad and it turned out that we both like to drink Dr. Pepper with pizza. It's a small world! I am glad to say that the pizza had a crisp, thin crust, good quality real dairy cheese and a strong, aromatic sauce. Also it was a tasty salad that wasn't all lettuce. Durinda agreed and asked if I would mind if she reviewed SaMo, too. I told her that would be great. She said that there are no great pizza places in Creswell, but the Capricciosa is as good as any she has had, even in nearby Eugene. I told her if she came back I would like to take her to Pizzana or Pizzeria Mozza, both really great gourmet pizza restaurants even though neither is on my Pico Boulevard crawl. We did agree that the plain décor at SaMo could use some sprucing up. It is so cool that Durinda and I seem to be agreeing on most things. It is, of course, true that we both have being Aspies in common, although we are different in many ways. For example, I am sensitive to loud noises and especially trumpet-like noises. She doesn't mind noises so much but is very sensitive when touching things like rough fabrics so she tries to wear soft fabrics and also certain kinds of fluorescent light can bother her. I am afraid neither of us have a great sense of humor because Asperger's people tend to be very literal thinkers, but I probably get jokes better than she does, although I haven't tested this theory thoroughly. I did ask her "Q: Why was the broom late? A: It overswept." She didn't think it was very funny, but I am not sure if that was because she didn't understand the joke or just didn't like it. Also, like most Aspies we both tend to dive really deep into certain subjects. I am very, very interested in airplanes, especially Douglas airplanes and she is very, very interested in fish. She has actually written an article about a zebrafish that was published in a journal of ichthyology. She has gone on trips all around the USA to study fish and once she went to Mexico. I am not as comfortable going places that aren't close to home but I think it is great that Durinda travels without worrying, especially to Los Angeles. Also she says she is interested in fixing cars and helps maintain the vehicles in her community. I was relieved that the pizza at SaMo was so good and that Durinda liked it.

CVS Drug Store—Wilshire Boulevard ★ ★ ★ ★

After eating some good Pizza at SaMo Pizza in Santa Monica, my friend Durinda, a Yelp Elite who is visiting from Creswell, Oregon, asked if she could meet my dog, Sadie. I have written about Sadie in several reviews and she is a wonderful dog. In order to spend time with Durinda while she is visiting Los Angeles, I left Sadie in her crate at home, but I have been worried about her for two reasons. She definitely would need to take a walk so she could poop and also I ran out of salmon oil which I give her with her food because she has an itching problem on her skin. Durinda said she would be glad to go with me to a CVS to get salmon oil. This was just a regular CVS like any other, but when I asked the woman at the checkout where I could find the salmon oil she knew right away and directed me to the correct aisle. I know it doesn't sound like a big deal, but it's unusual to get such good service at a CVS. When we got to the cash register Durinda said that the fluorescent lights were bothering her and that she would wait outside for me. There was someone ahead of me in line, and I wanted to hurry, but also I was trying to work out something in my head. I know I wanted Durinda to meet Sadie but also I think I was worried about what she might expect from me when we got to my apartment. She would be the absolute first girl outside of my sister, Lisa, coming to my apartment and I started focusing on whether Durinda would be expecting me to make some kind of move. If she sat on the sofa, should I sit on the sofa or the chair? Then I would worry if I put my arm around her that would be too soon but if I didn't, then she would think I didn't like her. I was actually starting to sweat, even though it wasn't warm in the CVS. I am embarrassed to say this, but just to avoid all of the stress that was creeping up on me, when I got to the parking lot I told Durinda that my place was a mess and I didn't want anybody to see it, but that if she waited outside I would bring Sadie out and we could go for a walk. If you know me, my place is never a mess. Fortunately Durinda said she didn't mind waiting.

In and Out Burger Los Angeles Airport ★ ★ ★ ★ ★ (Durinda's Review)

Out and Out wonderful! It bothers me to deviate from the format in my book like I did when I put in Durinda's letter a month ago, but Heather, my editor, thought readers would really like to see what Durinda wrote in Yelp about our visit to In and Out Burger. I found out later that Durinda wrote eight reviews for everything from the hotel to the airport shuttle while she was in Los Angeles, but the In and Out review is my favorite. I had to ask Durinda's permission if I could put it in my book and she said it was okay, so here it is:

In and Out Burger is a small but famous burger chain that started in Los Angeles and unfortunately hasn't yet reached Eugene, Oregon, where I live. I have heard they are known for their Double Double burger, which is two patties with cheese, tomato, lettuce and sauce. I am not going to tell you much more about the food except to say that I highly recommend that you go there if you haven't. I am going to take a cue from my friend Marcus who writes wonderful reviews from Santa Monica, California, and whom I am visiting with while I am attending a Yelp Elite event in Los Angeles. Marcus is unusual because he is very personal and revealing in his Yelp reviews and while it might make some people uncomfortable, he winds up being a very good communicator and will probably make Yelp Elite in record time, something that took me three years and over 800 reviews. He is a very interesting person who has decided to review every restaurant on a 15 mile long street in Los Angeles. So I am going to try to do a Marcus Katz style review and the cool thing is that Marcus Katz is in it. Together we had a pretty good pizza at Pico stop #13 on his journey, but afterward we picked up his dog, Sadie, and took her for a walk in his neighborhood. Sadie is a cute dog and Marcus is over the moon about her. I asked him where he might have chosen for us to eat if he didn't have to be on his Pico Boulevard trek. He then asked me if I had ever been "plane spotting" and I said no and he said that he would probably take me to In and Out by the airport for a Double Double burger and plane spotting which is one of his favorite things. He said that the In and Out by the giant Los Angeles airport is across the street from the runways where the big jets land and that people get their hamburgers to go and then walk across the intersection to a grassy area right next to the north runway. I asked if he would take me there anyway so I could see it. I know that Marcus is extremely shy, and even though I know about shyness myself, I would have to be bold and the one to ask. We had just eaten pizza, but I thought maybe we could go there for dessert. He said that they didn't have dessert, but we could have milk shakes that they make with real ice cream and we could act like that was dessert. When we got there it was totally amazing and I see why it is a favorite of his. The huge planes come so close overhead you feel like you could almost touch them and you can feel the ground shake when they land. It was night, but the planes had their landing lights on and the runway was lit as well, so you can see pretty well. Also, unlike Creswell, Los Angeles itself has so many lights that the city practically glows at night. There was a big line at the counter and Marcus got me a strawberry milkshake and he got a chocolate. My strawberry milkshake tasted like a real homemade milkshake with ice cream and not like a plastic McDonald's milkshake. Then we walked across a busy intersection to where maybe twenty or thirty people were hanging out, watching airplanes. Even though it was late, some of the parents brought their young kids. Some people had fancy cameras with big lenses, and some were listening on their cell phones to the voices on the control tower. I was afraid that Sadie would be bothered by the planes, but she wasn't. She is a very calm dog. Marcus seemed very excited when he saw what he said was a Qantas Airlines Airbus 380 come in from Sydney. It is a huge airplane, bigger than a 747. Do you know what an *airplane livery* is? I didn't. Livery is what aviation people call each airline's design and decoration on an airplane and to the plane spotters that's as important as or more important than the kind of plane. I always thought livery was just about horses. Marcus told me that ANA, which is a Japanese airline, has planes that are decorated to look like R2D2 and C3PO. We watched as a Norwegian Airlines 787 arrived from Oslo and Marcus told me that every Norwegian plane has a different hero painted on its tail. I couldn't tell, but Marcus said that it was the painter Edward Munch. Just off the top of his head, Marcus rattled off the Norwegian heroes like skater Sonja Henie, explorers Thor Heyerdahl and Roal Amundsen and the opera singer Kirsten Flagstad. What a brilliant idea! Now I want to fly on each of their airplanes! I admit I felt a little nervous standing on that little strip of grass with giant airplanes landing a hundred yards away, but having Marcus there made me more comfortable. I know he doesn't look like a movie star, but he has a sort of dignity and quiet presence that is hard to explain. And it is neat that he knows so much about airplanes. This In and Out is a very cool place and this is my longest Yelp review ever, even longer than most of Marcus' superlong reviews.

Resident's Court Hotel ★ ★ ★

This is a big hotel near the airport. I have passed it many times, but never had a reason to go in. I am just giving a quick impression of it as I am not actually a guest, but just dropping off my friend from Oregon, Durinda, who is staying there. Durinda is Yelp Elite and a very cool person who is going back to Oregon tomorrow. A sign by the driveway in front said "15 minute check-in parking only" so I pulled in there to say goodbye even though technically I wasn't checking in. Durinda asked me if I would walk her to the door. Inside she asked me if I wanted to come up, but I had already parked for a minute and a half and I didn't want to get a ticket so I said no. She suggested that we sit in the lobby for a few minutes and I could keep my eye on the time. I agreed and we sat down on a sofa for maybe a minute, kind of quiet, and Durinda asked me what kind of music I liked. I told her that I like bluegrass, jazz and classic rock, largely because my stepfather, Carl, plays them. I also said I like church and gospel music and that I have been a tenor in the Santa Monica First Congregational Church Choir even though I am Jewish. She asked me what my favorite gospel song is and I said it was "I Am a Pilgrim." I like this song especially because it is sung both in church and as part of the bluegrass repertoire and was made famous by the Kentucky Colonels, one of my stepfather's favorite bluegrass bands. Durinda said she didn't know it and asked if I could sing a little bit of it. It really sounds best when sung in close harmony, but Durinda insisted and I am kind of proud of my singing voice anyway so I sang the first verse. After I finished singing I only had two minutes left to get to my car. Durinda said that she really liked my voice and she thought I was a very smart and interesting person and she hoped we could stay in touch. Then she asked if it was all right if she gave me a kiss! I didn't know what kind of kiss she meant, but I was definitely up for whatever she had in mind. First she kissed me on the cheek like my mother used to, and then she put her hand on my neck and then she gave me a big, long, wet kiss on the mouth. I was really surprised, but then I had this amazing, deep, warm feeling well up inside me and I closed my eyes and kissed her back. Wow! Then I went back to my car with less than a minute to spare by my watch. I am not sure, but it is very possible I may be in love. By the way, I guess the Resident's Court is a perfectly good hotel. I didn't have a problem getting my car out and the sofa in the lobby was very comfortable. Although I never got to see Durinda's room, she said it was nice.

State of California Court Probate Division ★

Today was the day of my hearing with Judge Hughes in probate court to determine if I am going to be placed under an unwanted conservatorship. If Mother could know what was happening she would be very upset. I came with my stepfather, Carl, and his lawyer, Eleanor Sanchez. I had asked Carl to be my conservator after my scheming sister, Lisa, petitioned for conservatorship. After we went through entrance security we found the courtroom on the fourth floor and my court-appointed attorney, Frank Tuttle, was standing outside the courtroom door. I don't want him as my attorney, but I have no choice. He came over to say hello, but I didn't say anything back because I didn't want to say the wrong thing. I didn't see my sister, Lisa, but Eleanor pointed out a woman across the hall who she said was Lisa's attorney. Eleanor said she wasn't surprised that Lisa didn't have the nerve to show up after what she had started.

Although I don't think Lisa is lacking in nerve, I guess Eleanor is probably right. A court clerk opened the door and we all went in and waited for Judge Hughes to arrive and hear our case. I expected that he would be a gray-haired, judge-like older man, but when he came in he was only about forty with dark, wavy hair. On TV the judge is very often a black man and I once read it is because the networks want to hire more black actors and not make them play criminals all the time. There was a case before ours, but it was just a postponement and over in a few minutes. The judge had questions for each of the three attorneys. Lisa's attorney told the judge how I couldn't manage my budget and that I had gotten an apartment and car that I couldn't afford and was giving away large gifts irresponsibly. Eleanor told him that I had a good relationship with Carl and also that Lisa stood to benefit financially by limiting my spending. Also she made a point that Lisa apparently didn't care enough to even show up for the hearing. I thought Eleanor spoke very well. Frank Tuttle, who is supposed to be working for me, told the judge a bunch of hogwash that because of my limited financial understanding and my large resources I would be better off under a conservator. Eleanor warned me that he would probably say that because that way he could continue collecting fees as my court-appointed attorney and my estate would get billed for everything he did. Lisa's attorney then told the judge about how Carl didn't have much money when he met my mother and implied he was kind of a gold digger who was after my mother's money and would soon be after mine. Then she said that Carl made me buy him a fancy autopilot for his boat that cost three thousand dollars which I really couldn't afford. Carl didn't make me buy it at all. He asked me to return it when I gave it to him! That really made me mad and you could see how mad it made Carl although he knew better than to interrupt. Then the judge asked me some questions. First he asked me if I knew what the hearing was about—like he assumed I didn't have a working brain. That really made me angry and upset. At the time I think I may have been stimming which I sometimes do when I am stressed. For me that means rubbing my hands compulsively in a way that sometimes people notice and also I was probably swaying which people also find distracting. Considering I was totally aware that I could lose my freedom here, it was pretty hard to act calm and normal. But what was worse was I could feel something coming on inside me like a locomotive. If you are neurotypical, think about how it is when you know you are sick and are going to have to barf. You try to hold it in, but you can't, even though you try. I desperately didn't want to have a meltdown. Under the circumstances that would be really bad. Even though I felt there was a thunderstorm brewing inside me, I tried as hard as I could to keep it inside. I think Judge Hughes could tell that I was having a problem, and he spoke softly to try to make me feel better and asked what I would like to happen from the hearing. I told the judge that I really didn't want a conservator at all, but if I had to have one I wanted Carl. The judge asked me about the autopilot and I told him it was completely my idea to buy it for Carl for his birthday, but I don't know if he believed me. If he didn't that might mean that Lisa would be in charge of me. I'd probably lose my apartment and I might lose Sadie. He asked me if it occurred to me that it wasn't appropriate to give Carl such a big gift. Then I did a bad thing. I couldn't help it. But this was really a bad one. My face was probably all red. Then, much as I tried to keep myself in check, had a meltdown. Unlike some people farther along the spectrum, I don't have them very often, maybe a few times a year but I couldn't help this one. Everyone's meltdown is different, but for me I start flailing my arms around out of control and I will hit myself in the face with my palms. I know it must be scary for anyone around me even though I would never hurt anyone and have never really hurt myself. First the bailiff came up to me to try to do something, but I yelled at him and wouldn't let him touch me or even get near me. Then Carl came over and he tried to calm me down, speaking to me softly. He knew not to hug me or anything which some well-intentioned people might naturally do, but he just tried to keep me from hurting myself by talking to me. The judge asked Carl if he could take me outside and Carl managed to guide me into the hall where the bailiff followed and I slowly calmed down while I sat on a bench in the hall. The bailiff went back inside when he realized I wasn't going to hurt myself or anybody else. After a while Eleanor came out. First she looked to see how I was and I know I was definitely calming down. Then Carl excused himself and went over and talked to Eleanor on the other side of the hall. When he came back he looked pretty upset. When I asked him what happened he said that the judge had ruled that neither he nor Lisa would be conservators. He said that the judge had appointed some new person as temporary conservator. I asked him who that was. He said it was a professional conservator named Robert Casabian. Being a guardian was his business and he probably had many clients besides me. Carl didn't know anything about him. Eleanor came over and said that we could fight it. I didn't know what to think. I do believe that the judge made the wrong decision. He shouldn't have paid so much attention to that silly stuff about the autopilot and he should have known not to put me under so much stress that I had a meltdown. And he shouldn't have judged me by my actions for just a few minutes when almost all of the time I am perfectly okay. That is just not fair.

McCabe's Guitar Shop ★

McCabe's, which is in Santa Monica, is a famous place that not only sells guitars and musical instruments, but also has concerts in a room that holds about a hundred people. I am told that many famous musicians have played here including Elvis Costello and Linda Ronstadt. My stepfather, Carl, took me here last night to hear Bobby Allen who is a famous singer and guitarist with a big following in California because he grew up in Orange County. He was playing with his band and the concert had been sold out for several weeks according to Carl, but Carl and Bobby Allen are old friends, so not only did we get in, but we didn't have to pay $40 apiece. This was my first time at McCabe's, although I have been to several other music venues, mostly with Carl who has been a professional musician for most of his life and knows a lot of other musicians, some of them famous. In the 1980s Carl once played fiddle with Neil Young's band on tour. Bobby Allen's show at McCabe's included Bobby Allen and a backup band with bass guitar, rhythm guitar, fiddle and drums. They play in a kind of country and western/rock mode and the music was really good, although I thought it was a little loud at times. Bobby Allen's most famous song is called "Summer's Gone" and he sang it near the end of the show. The audience was very enthusiastic and they whooped and applauded during every song, but especially after "Summer's Gone." McCabe's doesn't have real theater seats, but they set up folding chairs in a large room that they usually use for demonstrating the guitars, banjoes and mandolins that are hanging on the walls and the chairs are not that comfortable and make you squirm. That is why I am deducting a star, even though I know this is a historic place with great ambience. When the concert was over, Carl brought me over to meet Bobby Allen. That is when Carl told me that Bobby had asked him to go with him on a tour of Sweden and Norway and that he would be leaving with the band next week.

Casa Los Toros Restaurant ★ ★

Tame tacos! Casa Los Toros is a slightly fancy Mexican restaurant. I say fancy because it has white tablecloths in the dining room and the waiters wear vests. It is not far from McCabe's where my stepfather, Carl, and I just saw Bobby Allen and his band play.

After the concert Bobby Allen and a few of the band members invited Carl (a very good musician) and me to join them at the bar at Casa Los Toros for Margaritas. I wasn't in much of a mood to go because Carl had just told me he would be leaving on tour in Scandinavia to play in the band with Bobby Allen. Because a judge had said I needed a conservator to watch my affairs, I was hoping it would be Carl who would do it but it didn't work out that way and what is worse is that now Carl was leaving altogether. Almost everyone in the band ordered a Margarita except me because I don't drink alcohol. I take medication and it is a hard enough task keeping my thoughts in control without adding alcohol. The waiter brought me some fish tacos which weren't Baja style and were just chopped up pieces of soggy fish with cilantro and onions on soggy flour tortillas. Pretty bad, especially for $14.50. I guess Carl knew I was unhappy because he was planning to go away just when I needed him and he spent time trying to talk to me even though I knew he would probably rather be hanging out with the guys from the band. One nice thing about playing an instrument really well is that you will always have other musicians you can hang out with. Carl said that it was probably the best thing for me that he was going away because he didn't think he was responsible or consistent enough to be my conservator and I would probably be better off with a professional who had experience and knew everything to do. I said that Eleanor, his attorney friend, had said she had a low opinion of conservators, but he said that Eleanor was always a glass-half-empty kind of person and I should probably at least start off with a positive frame of mind. He said he thought I had dodged the real bullet by avoiding getting Lisa as conservator. He promised he would stay in touch and he would be back in two months so it wasn't like forever. It seemed like forever to me. I think two stars is a fair rating for Casa Los Toros based on the fish tacos although maybe some other dishes are better there. I noticed that the Margaritas were big and nobody complained about them. Maybe I was in a bad mood because Carl was leaving. I will definitely miss Carl. I hope it goes okay with my conservator.

Robert Casabian Conservator ★

Robert Casabian came to my front door yesterday. The probate court has appointed him as my new conservator, but I wasn't expecting him. He seemed very friendly at first and said "Hello Marcus" like he was my best friend. Eleanor Sanchez, one of the attorneys involved in my ongoing conservatorship case in the probate court, warned me about people like Robert Casabian. Mr. Casabian told me that I needed to pack a suitcase right away because he was here to take me to a group home in Woodland Hills. He showed me a piece of paper which he said was a court order. I told him I didn't want to go to a group home. My sister had already tried to get me to go to a group home and I thought it was terrible. He said something about it being the best thing for me, but I wasn't having any of that and I told him that he had to leave right away. Then he said that I didn't have a choice, that the court gave him all the power to choose a residence for me, and that if I didn't come with him he would be forced to call the Santa Monica police and that they would put me in the mental hospital on a seventy-two hour psychiatric hold. This made me confused, angry and upset. He pulled out his phone and said that he was about to call the police and did I want that. I think I may have been crying at that point and I was trying desperately not to go into meltdown. Mr. Casabian said that if the police saw me like this they would certainly take me to the psychiatric ward and lock me in. I said I have a lot of things and I couldn't just pack them in a suitcase and he said that I just needed enough for a few days and that he would make sure an assistant got the rest of my stuff. Eleanor Sanchez, who is an attorney who has tried to be helpful had warned me that one of the things some conservators try to do is to drain your bank account, and one of the ways they do that is by hiring "assistants" to do little errands like going out for aspirin and charging your account fifty dollars an hour. Sadie, who is a very smart dog, barked at him. I asked Mr. Casabian if the group home allowed dogs as I wouldn't go anywhere without Sadie and he said that he was sure they did. He had his phone in his hand and asked me again if he needed to call the police and that it would be too bad because I would have an arrest on my record and that would make it very hard to get a job. I didn't totally believe what he was saying, but there was part of me that was worried that somehow he might be right. Then he started to act a little nicer and suggested I just go out and look at the group home with him. That seemed like a fair compromise so I said okay although I probably shouldn't have. Then he said again to pack a suitcase and I said I was just going to look, but he said that I couldn't tell unless I spent at least a few nights there or it wouldn't be a fair test. I said that I would pack a suitcase, but I wasn't guaranteeing him I would stay unless I liked it. He wanted to me to go in his car, but if he did that I wouldn't be able to get to my job at the Santa Monica library tomorrow afternoon and it is a long ways from Woodland Hills. He thought I should skip working for a day, but I have a perfect attendance record and would never skip my job unless I am very sick and that has never happened. Also I told him that I had a special pet car seat installed for Sadie and she only knows my car and likes to sit in the front in her seat. I told him I would follow him in my car with Sadie and that he could give me the address and I could put it in my GPS. At first he didn't want to let me drive, but then he gave in when I said it was the only way I would agree to go. It wasn't until after I had packed and gotten Sadie in the car that I told him we have to take Sepulveda Boulevard because I don't drive on the freeway which again didn't make him happy.

Woodland Vista Group Living ★ ★

I don't know what I expected when Robert Casabian, the man
that the probate court appointed against my will as conservator,
led me to the Woodland Vista Group Living Home. I was
there because Mr. Casabian was insisting that I move from
my apartment in Santa Monica, which I really like, to a group
home where more things would be taken care of for me. I'm
not stupid and I know it was all about money. The building
looked like a big old ugly stucco apartment house on a busy
street. I don't know why it was called Woodland Vista as there
were no woods and there was no vista that I could see, just cars
and trucks on Victory Boulevard and Valley smog. After we
both parked in the parking lot Mr. Casabian offered to help me
with my suitcase but he asked me to leave my dog, Sadie, in
the car until I checked things out. It was 75 degrees out when
we left Santa Monica, but now in the San Fernando Valley it
was about 90 degrees. He said I could leave the windows open
a crack but I told him there was no way I was going to leave
Sadie in the car. I put Sadie on her leash and we went inside. I
saw he had grabbed my suitcase out of the back seat and was
bringing it with him. There was a sort of a lobby, really just a
couple of broken-down old sofas and a scratched-up desk with
a telephone on it and nobody behind it. Mr. Casabian asked me
to wait so I sat on one of the sofas with Sadie next to me while
he went to look for somebody in charge. On a coffee table were
some business cards for takeout restaurants and a brochure for
Woodland Vista. I opened the brochure and it was sad how they
were trying to make the place look better in the photos than it
really did. It had pictures of a little round swimming pool in
the back and several young people swimming or sitting around
the pool like they were at some great resort in Waikiki. What
caught my eye was that there was a dog—a yellow Labrador
near the pool and one of the people was petting the dog. At
least there was a dog in the picture. That was when Robert

Casabian came back in the room with a woman who looked about forty and behind her was the same yellow Labrador that I saw in the picture. The woman had a big grin on her face as she walked up to me and said "Hello Marcus." It makes me uncomfortable when someone knows your name before you are introduced and you don't know theirs. Anyway, the yellow lab, who wasn't on a leash, immediately went over to Sadie who was sitting by my feet and started sniffing her butt. Sadie growled and I kept her leash tight. The woman introduced herself as Marianne and said the dog's name was Grace. She asked if I was comfortable with shaking hands so at least she was showing some awareness about the spectrum. I don't like shaking hands, but it's not a big issue for me. Then she started to say that Mr. Casabian had just told her about Sadie, but there had been a misunderstanding and she was sorry. She said Grace was an emotional support dog for everyone to share and get comfort from but they didn't allow residents to have personal dogs. It would have been good if I had known that before I came all that way with Sadie. I think she expected this would not sit well with me, but Robert Casabian immediately started to try to pretend that it was no problem. He went on in a really annoying way about what a nice dog Grace seemed to be and how great it would be that everyone in the group home could participate in taking care of her without having to take full responsibility for the dog and therefore freeing up time. He said that anyway it might be a hard transition for Sadie to make to have all of those people around and how she might be better off in a quieter environment. Somehow it didn't occur to him that both Sadie and I might be better off together in a quieter environment. All this conversation was interrupted when Sadie suddenly lunged and snapped at Grace and then Grace, who is twice Sadie's size, went back at her. I pulled Sadie away hard by her leash and Marianne grabbed Grace by the collar and yanked her. When the dogs were apart, Marianne said to Robert Casabian that she thought that it was already made clear in the Woodland Vista forms that residents could have tropical fish and turtles, but not dogs and he should have explained that to me. Robert turned to me and said something like he had tried his best and now I was going to have to give a little. That's when I knew that nothing was going to stop him from getting me deposited into Woodland Vista. I don't know what came over me but just on a flash of an idea I told him that I needed to take Sadie outside away from Grace and put her back in the car and then we could talk some more. When I got out the door I just ran with Sadie right to my car, jumped in and started it and took off fast from the parking lot. There was traffic in the street and just when it was clear enough to pull out, I heard a bang on the back of the car and I saw Mr. Casabian had pounded his fist on the trunk and was running up toward the car. I just hit the gas as he banged his fist against the car again. He yelled for me to stop and that I was going to regret it if I left. I didn't stop.

McDonald's (Woodland Hills CA) ★ ★ ★ ★

First let me apologize because I am writing this review on my Samsung Galaxy S10 cell phone and not my home computer as I usually do, and I am very upset, so I may make typing mistakes. Second, I don't think that any of my regular Yelp followers are waiting breathlessly for my review of a McDonald's in Woodland Hills, but this is where my dog, Sadie, and I landed after Robert Casabian, my new conservator, tried to make me move from my apartment into a creepy group home that wouldn't take my dog, Sadie. When he wasn't looking I grabbed Sadie and drove away. I am afraid to go back home to my apartment because Mr. Casabian has already threatened me with the police and I am afraid they will be waiting for me there. I ducked in here and parked in the back because I wanted to get off the street. I didn't trust my driving in my current state and I was afraid Mr. Casabian would try to chase after me in his car. I had to leave Sadie in the car while I went inside to order but now she's next to me at an outside table. I tried to reach my stepfather, Carl, but he is in Norway playing in a band and he doesn't answer his cell phone. Then I called my court-appointed attorney, Frank Tuttle, who seemed really ticked off when I told him what happened and he said that I had to contact Mr. Casabian right away and get myself back to the group home. He wanted to know where I was, but I wouldn't tell him and I hung up on him. Then I called Eleanor Sanchez, my stepfather's attorney who has been helpful to me in the past. She said that unfortunately Robert Casabian has a 100% legal right to determine residence for me which means he can send me to the group home or wherever he wants and there isn't much I can legally do about it. I told her that I couldn't go back to the group home without Sadie and I didn't see how anyone could make me. Eleanor said that my conservator has basically the same power as a parent of a minor and he can get the police to return me just like a runaway child. When I tried to talk more she said she was sorry, but she was my stepfather's attorney, not mine, and she couldn't offer me any more advice, but that she wished me well. Then I saw a police car pull into the parking lot and two policemen got out. I was afraid they were after me but then they walked right past me. Pheww! I guess I am now officially a fugitive. I will need to call the Santa Monica Library to let them know that I won't be there for work tomorrow. I feel bad about that and I hope they will forgive me. Also I really don't know where I can go. Because this is still officially a Yelp review, let me get business out of the way and say that I ordered a McFlurry with Oreos and M&Ms and a hamburger and a cup of water for Sadie. The food was okay and, like every McDonalds, as it should be. There were used food containers left on several of the outside tables, so I'm deducting for that. That's all for the review. Okay.

Note to readers from Marcus Katz:

Although I wrote the following reviews, because I became a fugitive, I did not post them in real time, but waited. I didn't want anybody, especially Robert Casabian to read them on Yelp and know where I was. Writing the reviews does make me calmer and helps me to think so I will keep writing even though I am not posting yet.

Walmart (Palmdale CA) ★ ★ ★ ★

Believe it or not, I have never been to a Walmart. There are no Walmarts anywhere near Santa Monica where I live. This is because real estate is expensive and people in Santa Monica prefer more upscale stores like Nordstrom and Bloomingdales. I needed a few shirts and some pants because I left Los Angeles in a hurry. There is a Target store in nearby Westwood that sells moderately priced clothes and sometimes I would go there although my late mother didn't like to shop there with me and insisted the clothes weren't well made. I am running from my conservator, Robert Casabian, and I don't feel it is safe to go home. Mr. Casabian wants me to live in a group home and separate me from Sadie, my dog. I have started driving north. I don't want to head south, toward Mexico because it is hot there and I don't speak Spanish and also I don't have a passport. I did have a thought that maybe I could go to Eugene, Oregon, where my friend (and woman of my dreams) Durinda Dowling lives. She recently invited me to visit her. But that is a long way (921 miles according to Google Maps) and I don't drive on the interstate so I would have to take mostly slower roads for most of the way. Also I am not comfortable driving at night, so I will have to find a place to stay before dark. Sunset is at 7:38 p.m. so I will try to find someplace by then. I have already gotten to Palmdale, thirty miles north of Los Angeles. I will keep going to get to route 395 that leads to Lake Tahoe and Reno. I hope that is far enough away that Mr. Casabian won't be able to follow me.

My voicemail now has seven calls from him and also two from my sister, Lisa. I have been thinking about calling Durinda, but I am working up to that and will probably wait until I get closer. I am worried she will tell me not to come and then what would I do? The Walmart is very big and full of people. Shopping for clothes is not hard because I like to wear basically the same thing every day—a dark or black polo shirt and chino pants, preferably Dockers. I found perfectly good cotton polo shirts for $7.87 each and bought three. I bought a pair of permanent press chino pants (not Dockers) in size 38x32, three pairs of cotton briefs and three pairs of black cotton socks, a gray sweatshirt and a windbreaker. I picked up a toothbrush, toothpaste and a disposable razor. I bought a cheap school backpack so I would have something to carry these things in. I also bought a tuna sandwich in a wrapper, kettle chips and an orange juice at the food stand on the way out. The sandwich looked pretty tired, but edible and I know I'm not in Santa Monica any more so I can't judge food by the same standards. I used my credit card for all of my purchases, but I did worry that Mr. Casabian might try to trace me through my credit card number. On the other hand it's not like I am a bank robber or anything and I don't think he would have the power to do that and in any case I think it would take him a while to get permission to try. Also I don't have any cash, so I really don't have much alternative.

Pilot Travel Center Victorville CA ★ ★ ★ ★ ★

Take me to the Pilot of your soul! The Pilot Travel Center is not like any gas station that I have ever been to. It is really a truck stop, with maybe twenty pumps and big tractor trailers all over the huge parking lot. You don't, however, need to be a trucker to go here. I needed gas on my trip north in Atomic Betty II, my 2011 Honda Civic, and gas was at least ten cents cheaper than the Chevron stations. They have a Dairy Queen and a Wendy's built right into the main building as well as a store that sells all kinds of snacks and drinks as well as things like hats and sunglasses. I got a Snickerdoodle Cookie Dough Blizzard at Dairy Queen. A Blizzard may not be the best food choice health-wise, but I am feeling blue, being cut off from home and being a fugitive at the moment and the Blizzard makes me feel a little bit better so I don't feel the least bit bad about not getting a salad at Wendy's. The girl who served me at Dairy Queen was named Jeanine, and although she is really cute with short blonde hair I am determined to be loyal to Durinda in Eugene. I know Durinda will be surprised to see me if I get there. I am still working up the nerve to call her to tell her I might be coming.

Timberland Motel (Lone Pine CA) ★ ★ ★ ★

I arrived at the Timberland Motel in the little town of Lone Pine at 7:56 p.m., about 8 minutes after sunset. I was trying to get there by sunset because I am not good at driving at night as the headlights from the opposite lane distract me. 7:56 is acceptable, however, especially because it takes about 80 minutes after sunset to get truly dark. It was distracting to have the setting sun come in through my side window, but Atomic Betty II, my Honda Civic, has a good visor and I was able to block out the sun for most of the time. I was afraid that there wouldn't be a room, but outside there was an old-fashioned sign that said "vacancy." In fact, everything was old-fashioned about the motel and that was just fine with me. Although I have traveled many places with Mother, the truth is I have never checked into a hotel or motel on my own. Not that it was difficult. Rosa, who was at the front desk, made it very easy for me. The room was $88 plus tax and they charged an extra $10 for bringing Sadie inside. I had to show her my credit card and my driver's license and they said they would charge my card if Sadie did any damage, but I wasn't worried about that. I was in room 17, which was on the second floor toward the back and away from traffic on route 395. Inside, the room smelled a little like mold and a little like bleach. There was an old-fashioned tube TV. I took in my bag with my clothes and toothbrush. I was really tired and I just kind of collapsed in a heap on the bed. I thought maybe this would be a good time to try to call Durinda, but I decided I was too tired and I might not make sense when I talked. I have never driven so far in one direction, 211 miles on my odometer, definitely a one-way record. Two years ago I drove back and forth from San Diego to attend Comic-Con, 256 miles, but that was both directions with a long stop between. I didn't want to get under the sheets because I didn't want to think about who might have last slept in the bed so I slept on top and Sadie slept on the floor next to me. The next thing I knew it was morning. That was when I realized that I hadn't brought my medication.

Big Pine Pharmacy ★ ★ ★ ★ ★

The one thing I forgot about when I left LA yesterday on a new adventure was my sertraline. I take 150mg of generic sertraline (also branded Zoloft) every morning. It helps me with my social anxiety although it isn't even close to being a cure, and also it helps me resist stimming, which in my case is wringing my hands or sometimes, when I am particularly anxious, rocking back and forth. My mother used to say that the Zoloft helped people to see the real Marcus. Not only does it help me, but if I stop taking my pill every day, I will feel some withdrawal symptoms. Strange things start happening inside my brain and sometimes I feel little electrical zaps that go from my head down my neck. Considering I am currently on the run from my conservator, Robert Casabian, and need to be at my mental best, I am afraid to be without it. If I were in Santa Monica now I could just go to my regular pharmacist and he would give me some pills to tide me over. Now that I am 211 miles from home in Lone Pine, California, which is near the base of Mount Whitney, the tallest mountain in California, I had a problem. When I walked into Big Pine Pharmacy it looked more like a souvenir shop than a pharmacy. The pharmacist's counter is way in the back. I didn't want to tell the pharmacist that I was running from my conservator, but I did tell him (his name tag said "Dick") that I had started on a trip and forgotten to take my Zoloft with me. Of course he wanted a prescription and when I said I didn't have one he said that he could call my doctor. I said my doctor was in Los Angeles and I wasn't sure if he would be able to reach her. Psychiatrists hardly ever answer their phone. I gave him the number anyway, although I didn't know how Dr. DeSantis would react if he managed to reach her. She would certainly wonder what I was doing in Lone Pine without my pills. After he dialed I guess he got her answering service and he left a message saying he was from Big Pine Pharmacy and her patient Marcus Katz was in the pharmacy and needed a prescription and could she fax it to the pharmacy. Then the pharmacist hung up and said that I could wait and see if she called back. I decided to wait for a bit and I looked around the shop. Besides being near Mount Whitney the store is also not far from the entrance road to Yosemite National Park and near Mammoth Mountain Ski Area and there are mugs and stuffed animals and key chains everywhere to sell to people passing through. I found a really funny little plaque that said *Around here I am a very responsible person. Every time something goes wrong I am responsible.* I thought that if I do decide to travel to see Durinda (I am leaning in that direction now), I could get it for her but I am not sure about her sense of humor. The pharmacist called my name and said that Dr. DeSantis was on the phone and wanted to talk to me. My first fear was that Dr. DeSantis wouldn't be around to write my prescription. My second fear was that I would have to talk to her and tell her that I was on the run. I picked up the phone and I knew what she was going to say because she always says it when I come into her office. "Tell me what's happening with you, Marcus." I wanted to tell her everything, but I kind of got stuck. Then she said, "Why are you in Lone Pine?" So I let loose. I told her about Robert Casabian and about Woodland Vista and about how I felt like I was being made a prisoner and about how this was all about money and I didn't even care about the money. I just wish things could go back the way they were. I was sure she would tell me in some calm and even-handed way to come back, but she didn't. She said that she didn't know if what I was doing was the best thing, but that she really didn't think I needed a conservator and that she hoped that I could work it out and that she would help me in any way she could. She said that her biggest worry was that I would cut myself off from the people who know and care about me. She asked me to stay in touch with her wherever I was and that I could tell her anything because our conversations were privileged and couldn't ever be used in court. (I already knew that from watching *The Sopranos* except I believe if she thinks I am going to murder someone she has to tell the police.) She said she would fax a prescription right away and again she asked that I get in touch with her for any reason. It took about ten minutes for Dr. DeSantis to fax the prescription and another ten for the pharmacist to fill it. When he gave it to me he wished me good luck and said he heard what I had to say to Dr. DeSantis and he didn't understand why I should have a conservator either. He asked if someone would come looking for me and I said I didn't know.

Mountain AAA Towing and Service ★ ★ ★ ★ ★

I was driving Atomic Betty II, my 2011 Honda Civic, on route 395 in northern California on my way perhaps to Eugene, Oregon. I hadn't decided definitely whether I would go to Eugene although I was certainly headed in that direction and there was someone that I definitely needed to call if I was going to go there because one shouldn't show up at a doorstep 912 miles away without some advance warning. I have been counting mile markers. It keeps my mind occupied and not thinking so much about Robert Casabian, my conservator, who was probably trying to find me right now. Mile marker numbers usually go up from south to north. It would be nice if they just counted up from the very beginning of the highway so you knew exactly how far you had traveled but they often start at county lines. I was in such a bad state of mind when I first left Los Angeles that I didn't set my trip meter on Atomic Betty II. I can calculate the miles on Google Maps, but it's not as much fun as a trip odometer and nowhere near as interesting as counting mile markers. I had just passed mile marker R55.7 which is in Lassen County, California, famous for its volcanic lava formations, when an animal ran out in front of me. I think it was either a big squirrel or maybe a little fox, but it happened so quickly I didn't get a good look at it. I swerved right away. Fortunately there weren't any other cars near me, but I wound up skidding off to the side of the road and my tire hit a big rock before stopping. When I tried to back up, the steering felt funny and the car wouldn't back up straight. I got out and saw my right front tire was flat. I have never changed a tire and I looked in the glove compartment for a booklet to show me what to do, but there wasn't one. I decided to Google "changing a tire" as cars and trucks whizzed past when a beige pickup truck pulling a horse trailer pulled over just in front of me. A brown-skinned man, with lots of tattoos, dressed in old blue jeans, cowboy hat and boots got out of the truck and walked toward me and asked if I needed help. I said I had a flat tire and I would try to fix it myself, but he came over and looked at the wheel and shook his head. He said that my front suspension was bent and that the car would need to be towed and there was a mechanic in Bishop, which was about four miles north. It's a good thing that I had managed to get Zoloft in Lone Pine. My dog, Sadie, who was still in the car, started barking. I excused myself and took her out on her leash so she wouldn't run out on the highway and she immediately pulled me toward the horse trailer where there was a horse inside. Sadie sniffed around the horse who was agreeable to that. The man asked what my dog's name was. I told him "Sadie" and he said his horse's name was Sargento and that his name was Francisco. He asked me if I was an auto club member because I would have to call a tow truck. I still have my mother's AAA card, the same one I had to use when the first Atomic Betty, my old Mercedes died, and I can't believe I had to use it again so soon. I called and the operator said someone would be out in fifteen minutes. Francisco asked if I would be all right. I thanked him and he left. The tow truck came in twelve minutes and brought me and Atomic Betty II straight into Bishop and dropped me off at the mechanic's garage.

RJ's Auto Service (Bishop CA) ★ ★ ★ ★ ★

After I accidentally hit a rock on the side of the road and got a flat tire and some kind of damage to the wheel, the AAA towed my car to Bishop, a small town that's near the Mammoth ski area. RJ's Auto Service is just off the main road. R.J., the owner, is a man in his forties in a gray coverall who just looked like he knew everything about fixing cars. Of course I checked his Yelp reviews and he has 33 reviews averaging 5 stars. Thank you Yelp! He put my Honda, Atomic Betty II, on the hydraulic lift and took off the front wheel with the flat tire. He looked underneath the front end and shook his head. He said that the front suspension control arms and steering arm were bent and also I needed a new backing plate. I don't know exactly what all these things are, but I could see things looked bent up in there. Also he said I would need a new tire and wheel. He told me he would have to order the parts and he wouldn't be able to have Atomic Betty fixed until the next day and it would cost about $850. Ouch! He said that he needed a deposit before ordering the parts. I gave him my Wells Fargo Visa card and he swiped it on the little machine in his office. After swiping it twice he told me that the bank had refused the card and asked if I had another card. That surprised me. I told him I had just used it at the pharmacy in Lone Pine. Then I gave him my Wells Fargo debit card and after I put in my pin number it was also refused. He suggested I call the number on the card which I did right away. I got put on hold by two people, but the last person told me that my account had been suspended due to a court order. I asked him what court, but he said he didn't know. He asked if I had received a notice in the mail and I said that I hadn't been home for two days. I was getting a really bad feeling. Then I called Emma at Northwestern Trust who is the trustee of my mother's trust. She said she didn't know anything about what happened to my credit card, but it is likely that Robert Casabian, the man who was appointed by the probate court to be my guardian had court permission to manage my accounts. She asked if I was having a problem with Mr. Casabian and I told her that he had tried to put me in a bad group home against my will and that I had run away. She urged me to come home because she didn't think that running away could possibly help my cause. I know it is not her fault what is happening to me, but I don't think coming home is going to solve anything. I needed some time to think. RJ said that he would keep Atomic Betty for me until I figured things out and he wouldn't charge for storage. I had considered calling my friend Durinda in Eugene, Oregon, but then I thought that it would be bad if I called her to say that I needed money. I decided to take Sadie for a walk and get something to eat and try to clear my head. I had $58 in my wallet as well as the useless credit card. My phone rang while I was walking and I answered it. It was my sister, Lisa. She said that a private detective had just come to their house looking for me and that there was an arrest warrant out for me and the detective wanted to know where I was. She said I should come home right away. I didn't know whether to believe her. I said I can't believe my conservator would really hire a private detective. Lisa said that they would and that they did and that his fees would be paid out of the estate and that Mr. Casabian gets an additional 20% fee for hiring him and his incentive is to spend as much money as possible in my account until there is none left and it was all my fault for not letting her be guardian. That was very disturbing, but I didn't tell her where I was. I said goodbye and shut off the phone.

El Patio Mexican Restaurant (Bishop CA) ★ ★ ★

Mi taco es su taco. I was walking down the main street in downtown Bishop with my dog, Sadie, trying to get my head clear. I was stuck in Bishop after I had been told by a mechanic that my car, Atomic Betty II, needed $850 worth of repairs and my credit card had been frozen by my new conservator. I was a little bit hungry but also needed to make the $58 in my wallet last. For how long? That was what I didn't know. Maybe forever. Or maybe just until I gave in to Robert Casabian, my conservator, who apparently has obtained a police warrant for me. As I walked past El Patio Restaurant, a storefront restaurant, there was a little patch of grass for Sadie. I recognized a parked truck with a horse trailer at the curb. It belonged to Francisco, the man who offered to help me when my car broke down this morning. I went over and patted his horse, Sargento, through the slat in the trailer. Sadie seemed happy to see Sargento, or really to smell him because she couldn't quite see him from where she was. When I looked up I saw that Francisco was sitting at a table by the window in El Patio, waving at me, so I tied Sadie's leash around a newspaper box by the door, told her to wait and went inside. Francisco was by himself, sipping a Corona. He asked me how my car was. He seemed like he had been there drinking for a while and insisted I sit down and have a beer with him. I told him I don't drink, but then he offered to buy me a hamburger and that sounded pretty appealing even if this was a Mexican restaurant. The hamburger was just okay, a little dry, and the bun was stale. (That's all the review, folks, because my own circumstances are more on my mind than food for now.) He asked if I got my car fixed and somehow, even though he was just a drunken stranger, I guess I needed to unload. I wound up telling him the whole story of how I was running away and that Robert Casabian had frozen my credit card and has the police looking for me. He laughed kind of a sixth beer laugh and said something about how when the white people can't find any more brown people to screw over they move on to other white people. Francisco said I needed a plan. I told him I didn't really have a plan, but that I hoped to get up to Eugene because I have a friend up there. He said he was on his way to Reno to participate in an Indian rodeo. He told me he is part Mexican and part Paiute Indian and his specialty is tie-down roping which some people call calf roping and that he once won a $10,000 prize at a rodeo in Albuquerque. I said that it was cool to meet a real rodeo cowboy. Francisco said he wasn't a real cowboy and he makes his living installing HVACs, but he likes the calf-roping event and Sargento is a very good horse with natural rodeo instincts. He said first he was going to stop along the way at the Walker River Paiute reservation to visit some cousins. Francisco said that if I was so worried about the police, I would be immune from arrest on the reservation. Considering there were no alternatives, it sounded tempting. After we sat a while and he had one more beer he told me he knew he had probably drunk too much and he was not in good shape to drive. He asked me if I would drive the truck and trailer and then I could stay with his cousins while I was there. I wasn't sure about this for several reasons, first being I have never driven a truck, let alone a truck with a horse trailer. While Francisco had been very kind to me already, I don't know what to think of a man who would allow himself to get so drunk when he knew he had a lot of driving ahead of him. Also I didn't want to just leave Atomic Betty II. Francisco said that I could do what

I wanted, but that for somebody who is a long way from home and scared about the police, it sounded like he was offering a good deal. I decided that he was right and this was my best option. I looked up Walker River Reservation on Google Maps and while it is not on a direct route to Eugene, Oregon, it does carry me north and north is away from Mr. Casabian and the group home. Nobody has to remind me that I am putting off calling my friend Durinda in Eugene and let her know about my situation. I don't know why that is so hard to do and I am embarrassed that I can't bring myself to do it.

Traveler's Lodge and Campground (Hawthorne NV) ★ ★

This is not a Travelodge, but a "Traveler's Lodge." I know that a regular Travelodge is not super classy, but this is definitely less than that. When I was younger and sometimes traveled with my mother to San Francisco or New York we always stayed in really nice hotels. When I was five and she and my father were still married, I remember we stayed at the Fairmont Hotel in San Francisco on the top of Knob Hill where the lady at the front desk gave me Lindt chocolate and I slept on a rollaway bed. My father wanted me to have a separate room, but both my mother and I didn't want me to sleep alone in a strange place. The room at the Traveler's Lodge was very plain and had two beds, a TV on the wall and a wash basin on the outside of the bathroom near the entry. I should have let Francisco know that I don't drive at night when he first asked me to drive his truck after he had too many beers to drive. If I had told him that I needed to stop driving at dark, he might not have drunk two more beers in the truck along the way while I drove. (Having an open beer bottle in the car made me nervous anyway, but Francisco said he would empty the bottle in the unlikely event a policeman stopped us.) I have a problem with lights from oncoming cars flashing in my eyes and I get disoriented and sometimes nauseous at night. In the daytime and even up to twilight, driving the truck and trailer, a dirty red Ford pickup truck with a trailer behind was actually exciting after I got over my nervousness. The truck was really high off the ground and looking at the trailer in the big side mirrors made me feel like I was an engineer driving a train. Then the sun started to set. Francisco was not happy when I told him I was going to need to stop driving. He said that he didn't want to keep Sargento in the trailer for an extra night and threatened to drive himself the 100 miles to the reservation even though he was in no condition. I told him that Sadie and I would definitely have to get out if he did that. He relented and said that we would spend the night in a motel and leave at dawn. Later we could go on to Reno where he had to register and pay his entry fee for the rodeo where he was going to compete. We had turned off of 395 onto route 95 which is a lonely desert road. At the little town of Hawthorne there were two choices, and the Traveler's Lodge was the cheaper of the two with a sign out front that said $57 a night with cable TV. I felt bad that Francisco had to pay for me as my credit card was now blocked. The hotel clerk said that dogs weren't allowed in the room and that Sadie would have to sleep in the truck and she better not bark and wake up any of the guests. Francisco told the clerk that was okay, but then on the way to the room after registering, he said that we would just sneak Sadie into the room no problem. When we got to the room Sadie didn't like it there and started scratching at the door to get out. Also, Francisco smelled of beer and sweat and the carpets stank of smoke and ammonia, so I took a pillow and blanket from the motel and told Francisco that I would rather sleep in the truck with Sadie, which I did, taking some time to pet Sargento who was stuck alone in the trailer which I guess was partly my fault for not being able to drive at night.

Summertime Smoke Shop (Schurz NV) ★ ★ ★ ★

My rodeo cowboy companion Francisco and I arrived around noon in Schurz, Nevada, on the Walker River Paiute Indian reservation. The landscape all around is scrub and desert. I can't tell you why a Native American town has a German sounding name and Francisco didn't know either. It really isn't a town, just a few buildings, like the town hall and the police department, a fix-it shop, four fireworks stands made of converted shipping containers and the Summertime Smoke Shop which isn't really a smoke shop although they do sell cigarettes. The Summertime Smoke Shop is more like a 7–11 or a general store. It's a cinderblock building with two gas pumps out in front and inside they sell groceries and home items and tools and everything else one might need in the several hundred homes on the reservation. Francisco says that there is a Walmart forty miles north in Fallon, but this is where the Walker River Paiutes get milk and eggs, bread, soda and beer. Inside the store is clean and everything is neatly displayed. Francisco, who is part Paiute, was thankfully sober and he drove this morning. He pulled in front of the pumps to get gas, telling me that gas is cheap on the reservation because the tribe doesn't have to pay state gas taxes. I followed him when he went inside and picked out a twelve-pack of Budweiser that he said was for his aunt and uncle who we would visit shortly. The woman behind the counter, who appeared to be Native American, knew Francisco and called him by his name. He grabbed a Dr. Pepper for me as he had already found out that was my favorite soda, and picked out a couple of wrapped bean burritos from the refrigerator, handing me one. He paid her for the gas and the food. The burrito was surprisingly good (maybe because I was hungry) and she was very polite. Francisco asked the woman if "Walter" was around and she said that she had seen Walter's car in front of the tribal office.

Walker River Paiute Tribal Police ★ ★ ★ ★ ★

While we were on the Paiute Reservation in Schurz, Nevada, my new friend, Francisco, insisted that I visit with Walter Smith, the chief of police for the reservation to try to sort out my legal troubles. By the way, if you think Schurz is a strange name for a reservation town, most of the Native Americans here have last names of Smith and Washington and Wilson. I was expecting a name like Running Bear or Shining Water or something like that, but I guess that the white man must have got them to change their names sometime in the past. I was pretty nervous about going into the police station, but Francisco assured me that Walter is a very good person to talk to and that they were friends from childhood. Walter, who looked to be about fifty, wore a police uniform and spoke in a slow and deliberate way. Francisco told him how I had run away from a conservator who was trying to steal my inheritance (he may have embellished a little) and that I was a good young man who could use some help. Walter first asked me if there was a warrant out for me. I told him that I thought my sister, Lisa, said something about a warrant, but I don't completely trust Lisa so I wasn't sure. Walter asked to see my driver's license which I gave him although I was a bit reluctant under the circumstances. He went on their computer and after a minute said there was something called a "writ of assistance" which meant the court was looking for me and then he asked me if I had hit anyone with my car. I said that I hadn't hit anybody with my car ever. Then he asked if I ever graduated high school and if I took any drugs. I guess he was just trying to size me up. I told him that I had a certificate from Santa Monica College, a two-year program, and the only drug I take is my Zoloft. He asked if I could support myself and I explained that before I left I had my SSDI payments and my part-time wages from working at the Santa Monica Library and that my mother had left me quite a bit of money and that was the problem because both my conservator, Mr. Casabian, and my sister, Lisa, were trying to get at it. I told him that Francisco said I was safe while I was on the reservation and he said that Francisco was right about that, and he would give me the benefit of the doubt and not hold me on the warrant, but there was no way I should stay on the reservation. He said he couldn't imagine how I could ever live in Schurz or on a reservation for more than a few days if I'm used to living in Los Angeles. I knew he was right. He also said the police probably wouldn't really be out searching for me, but if I got arrested or detained for an infraction, even jaywalking, the police would run my ID through the system and find the warrant. Then they would certainly arrest me. He said that if it's true that there is a bunch of money involved, that greedy people might hire a private detective or a bounty hunter to try and find me. He asked if I had a cell phone. I showed him my Samsung and he said I should get rid of it and buy a new phone. He asked if I was using credit cards because that is an easy way to track someone and I said that my Wells Fargo bank account and credit card had been frozen. He said that was probably a lucky thing because it would make me harder to find. Walter asked me what I planned to do for money and I said I had about forty-five dollars left. He asked if I had any other bank accounts besides Wells Fargo, maybe one I had forgotten about, and I was about to say no when I realized that the money that I earn from the Santa Monica Library is deposited directly into the Santa Monica Public Employee Credit Union where I transfer it into my Wells Fargo account. He asked if that account had been blocked by my conservator. I didn't know but Walter let me sit in front of his computer while I tried to access my account with my password (*Ameliaearheart1937* but don't bother to try to use it because I have changed it). It worked. The screen said I still had $277 in the account! I think Francisco was relieved because it meant that he might not have to keep paying for me. But I didn't have an ATM card to access it and the credit union office is in Los Angeles. How would I get at the money? With Walter's help I managed to wire the money to the nearest Western Union office which was in Reno. Although $277 is not going to last forever, at least I have a little bit to keep me going. And thanks so much to Chief Walter Smith and the Walker River Tribal Police! Very kind and very helpful!

Big Chief Fireworks Company (Schurz NV) ★ ★ ★ ★ ★

After getting some helpful information about my current situation from the chief of police, I was walking to the car with my friend Francisco when I noticed a ragged old teepee and an orange cargo container with an open door and signs hanging everywhere advertising fireworks. I guess fireworks are a good business for a community which is obviously very poor. Francisco asked me if I liked fireworks and I said I did, although I like looking at them more than hearing them. There used to be a Fourth of July fireworks display near the amusement pier in Santa Monica but years ago the city council decided that it was bringing too many rowdy people into town and they stopped. Francisco asked me if I had ever set off my own personal fireworks (not just sparklers) and I told him that I hadn't because they are illegal and dangerous. Of course there are always some teenagers setting off fireworks in the neighborhoods the week before the fourth, but I never got asked to take part and I am sure Mother wouldn't have allowed it. We went inside the open door of the cargo container and hundreds of colorful fireworks assortment boxes with names like "Rolling Thunder" and "Aerial Barrage" were arranged neatly in the aisles. I guess Francisco knows everybody in Schurz, because he introduced me to Amber, a member of the tribe, who was in charge. She asked if I was in the rodeo, too, but I don't know if she was serious or kidding me because I don't look anything like a cowboy. I did say no. She asked me what kind of fireworks I liked, but I didn't know how to answer because

I don't know much about fireworks and I didn't think we were buying any, but Francisco surprised me when he bought a big box assortment called "Space Fire." The label said that it had bottle rockets, flying novelties and fountains. I don't know what a flying novelty is, but I guess I will find out. Amber was really nice and although Teepee Fireworks is my first fireworks store ever it seemed very well run with a lot of choices so I am giving it five stars. If you are interested, I should mention that after Teepee we visited Francisco's cousin and her husband on the reservation, Sandra and Eddie. They have four children and the youngest, Ruby and Robert, were helping Sandra in their garden. They lived in a mobile home about six miles east of Schurz on a big plot of desert land with three horses and some chickens. They were happy to see Francisco and asked him questions about the rodeo and some family things while drinking the beer that Francisco had brought. I learned that Francisco was separated from his wife and had two small children. I know that these are things I probably should have learned about him while we spent so much time together, but I think I am not good at making conversation. Sandra made us some bologna and cheese sandwiches to take on the road and then we left because Francisco had to check in for the rodeo before 4 p.m. Francisco drove.

Western Union (Reno NV) ★ ★ ★

My friend Francisco and I finally made it to Reno after two days on the road from Bishop, CA. Francisco, who is a rodeo rider, registered his entry at the rodeo grounds at the edge of town and dropped off his horse, Sargento, at the stable. I helped back Sargento off the trailer. Then Francisco showed me how to brush him, starting with a grooming mitt and circular motions and then stroking with a brush. Sargento was very calm and seemed to like it when I brushed him. I have never been to a rodeo and am looking forward to seeing Francisco and Sargento tomorrow where they will compete in the calf roping contest. Francisco has signed me in as his helper which means I won't have to buy a ticket. Before we checked in at a motel Francisco said we should take care of my business. I needed to go to a Western Union office to pick up some much needed cash ($277) that should have been transferred from my credit union account. One of the good things about being in Reno, which is a center of gambling and casinos, is that there are loads of Western Union offices and there was one directly on the way to our hotel. I have never been to a Western Union office, but this one is a small storefront with a man behind a thick plastic window that looks like it was built to resist bullets. You show them two forms of ID and they look on the computer to see if they have cash in their system for you. Although the man wasn't very polite (it occurred to me because he didn't look at me directly that maybe he was Aspie, too, but I decided he was just not social), he did find me in the computer and printed out a money order and handed it to me. I expected cash, but he said that he could cash it for a $4 fee. I cashed it although I didn't like having to pay the $4. I got two $100 bills and the rest in twenties, a ten, and three ones. While that is more than I am used to carrying in my wallet, I am still worried that it won't sustain me for very long in my current situation, which is being a fugitive from a conniving conservator in Los Angeles. A fugitive has a lot of expenses.

Cellular World (Reno) ★ ★ ★ ★ ★

Because my evil conservator, Robert Casabian, is for sure trying to find me and take me back to Los Angeles, I need to get rid of my cell phone and get a new "burner" phone. Burner phones are surprisingly cheap and with my friend Francisco's help, I found one at Cellular World in Reno for just $79 including 1gigabyte of data, 1000 texts and 1000 minutes of talk time which is more than I ever talk on the phone in a lifetime. The salesman at the store was Jason and he was very helpful, showing me all the features of the new LG phone. All phones look pretty much alike to me although I know this phone is a much less fancy phone than my old Samsung. I asked if they would buy the Samsung and when he put in the battery and turned it on (I had shut it off and removed the battery so I couldn't be found) he looked at it and told me that I had several unopened voicemails and asked if I wanted to listen to them. I looked at the messages and three were from my sister, Lisa, and one was from a Los Angeles (310 area code) number that I didn't know. I excused myself from Jason and Francisco and listened to the messages. The ones from Lisa were just her telling me again and again that I was making a mistake and I should return home. The other turned out to be from Robert Casabian. Like Lisa, he also said that I should return home, but he also said that if I didn't contact him or come home right away he would assume that I was mentally imbalanced and when I was found, which was certainly going to happen because I can't hide forever, he would have me committed to a psychiatric facility. When I finished listening I pulled out the battery right away. Jason said they could offer me $25 for the phone which I would have taken because I only had about $198 left after buying the phone, but Francisco said it wasn't enough for a nice phone and suggested I keep it for now. Jason showed me all of the features of the new phone, which was similar to my old one because they both use the Android operating system.

Players Motel (Reno NV) ★ ★

My friend Francisco is going to compete in the calf roping event at the rodeo in Reno tomorrow. He booked a room at the Players Motel in Reno and left his horse, Sargento, at the rodeo grounds stable. Players Motel is close to the rodeo grounds and, according to Francisco, many of the rodeo riders stay there. Also, according to Francisco, it is reasonably priced compared to other motels around. The room was very basic and I did see black mold on the edge of the tub where it met the floor in the bathroom, but other than that it seemed pretty okay. I think since I started on my trip my standards are changing. Maybe that's a good thing. I don't know. Francisco and I have been on the road together in his pickup truck for two days since we got together in Bishop, CA. When we stayed at another motel last night in Hawthorne NV, I wound up sleeping in the truck, partly because the motel didn't allow dogs and my dog, Sadie, would have had to break the rules to stay. This motel does allow dogs, but I have to admit that I'm not very good at sleeping with another person in the room and although Francisco is a very good man his hygiene is not that great. I really don't have enough money to get a room of my own. I asked Francisco if he minded if I slept in the truck again with Sadie. I was afraid I was going to hurt his feelings by not wanting to stay in the room with him. He said he was going to hang out with some of his cowboy buddies and maybe go out and do a little drinking with them and I could stay in the truck on one condition — that I call my friend Durinda in Eugene, Oregon, and tell her that I was coming there. He said it wouldn't be right to just show up, assuming that I even worked up the nerve to make it there. That was all a bit of a surprise and I told him I didn't think that was his business. He said that he was making it his business and if I wanted to stay I had to promise him. I know he was right and I know what he was saying was in my best interest, but I really didn't want to call right then. Around nine o'clock some other rodeo cowboys stopped by the room carrying beer in paper bags. Francisco left with them and said he was going to go see some old friends in another room upstairs. He didn't ask me to go, but that was okay because I stayed in the room with Sadie and watched *Jeopardy* and *Big Bang Theory*. After a while I heard Francisco calling my name from outside the room. I opened the door and he was standing there with three other men and a girl. They all had beers in their hands and were laughing and Francisco said it was time to set off fireworks. He said to leave Sadie in the room because dogs don't like fireworks. Everybody went over to the edge of the parking lot near a field and Francisco opened the fireworks box. First he pulled out a fountain and put it on the ground and he held out a butane lighter and said I should light it. I have never lit fireworks and the idea made me nervous. But he insisted and everybody else said I should just do it, so I did. I touched the lighter to the fuse and ran back and after a couple of seconds there was a big spray of gold and blue sparks and it made a whistling noise. His friends all congratulated me and I was surprised how exciting it was. I wanted to light another one, but Francisco lit the next one which was a bottle rocket that he launched out of an empty beer bottle and it took off with a whizzing sound and went about a hundred feet in the air. Then he set off a few more bottle rockets and then there were two Roman candles. He lit one and held it in his hand and pointed it at the sky. It shot five or six blue and green fireballs in the air. Then he lit the other one and he handed it to me. OMG! It shot out a bunch of fireballs with a big whooshing sound and I could feel them shooting out of the tube. It was totally cool. I turned around and a bunch of people were looking down at us from the balcony of the motel. Then we started on the firecrackers including a couple of strings of ladyfingers that made a lot of noise. Then a police car pulled into the parking lot with its lights flashing and right away Francisco's friends took off leaving just me and him. A policeman stepped out of the car and asked us if we knew that fireworks are illegal there. Francisco said he was sorry and that we would stop. Then the policeman asked us for our ID. This is a <u>very big problem</u> because if he ran my license in his computer he would probably find out that there is a warrant for me in Los Angeles. Francisco got out his license and the policeman looked at it with his flashlight. Francisco apologized again and said he was here for the rodeo. The cop said that he should know that fireworks could start a fire or injure someone. I was getting my license out when Francisco said the fireworks belonged to him alone and I was just here watching, but the policeman wanted to see it anyway. He looked at it with his flashlight and looked at my face to see if it matched. He asked what I was doing here and Francisco said I was here to watch the rodeo. I think I may have started stimming and rocking, maybe moaning and acting generally weird because I was really scared that this would mean I would go to jail and be sent back to court in Los Angeles and then a group home and maybe even a psychiatric hospital according to Mr. Casabian. I may even been crying a little bit. The cop asked if Francisco and I were related even though we don't look at all alike and Francisco said no and then he took the licenses and I think he was going back to his car probably to check if there were warrants when Francisco said that I was a little bit retarded and that the policeman was scaring me and could he please give us a break. Retarded? That hurt my feelings a lot coming from someone who should know better although it is not the first time a perfectly intelligent Aspie has been called that or worse. On the other hand, the policeman stopped walking, looked us up and down and gave us our licenses back and told us to clean up the fireworks debris. We did, but I told Francisco that it was a really bad thing to get me in trouble with the fireworks and then he shouldn't have called me retarded. Francisco said that he just told the policeman that so he wouldn't run my license. He didn't mean any harm. Then he asked me if it was really the truth that I hadn't hit anybody with my car back in Los Angeles which hurt my feelings all over again. Of course I told him that I hadn't and it was probably a way for Robert Casabian to get back at me. If all of that wasn't bad enough, when I got back into the room Sadie was sitting in a corner, whimpering and shivering after having been scared by the noise of the fireworks outside. I should have known they would scare her and I felt terrible. I held her close and took her into the truck where we spent the night which was fine because I didn't like this motel anyway.

Denny's (East Reno NV) ★ ★ ★ ★

A Denny's is a Denny's. I have eaten before at the Westwood Denny's near my home in Santa Monica, CA. I think Denny's serves the same menu everywhere. I had breakfast at Denny's in East Reno with my traveling companion, Francisco, who is going to be in a rodeo today with his horse, Sargento. This Denny's was very clean and efficient. Our server, Rosa, was polite and brought my Grand Slam breakfast (two eggs, sausage, hash browns and two buttermilk pancakes) quickly and it was hot. She kept my water glass filled and brought me extra syrup for my pancakes. The restaurant was walking distance from the motel where Francisco and I stayed last night. Actually, I stayed in Francisco's truck and he stayed in the motel. Yesterday was not a good day because I nearly got arrested by the Reno police for fireworks and it was mostly Francisco's fault because he had too much to drink and exercised bad judgment. This morning he said he was sorry for what happened. He also asked if after the rodeo I was still going to visit my friend Durinda who lives in Eugene, Oregon. He wanted to know if I had called her like I promised I would. I said I didn't and he said he didn't even believe there was a Durinda and that I was making it up. I told him there was and that she even kissed me once. He said that if I didn't call her right then I couldn't come to the rodeo and he would just leave me there. I didn't believe him, but then he started for the door. I knew he was right. Francisco stood there while I dialed. I thought maybe she won't answer because she is at work. But she did answer and Francisco left me alone so I could talk to her. When I told her who it was she said she was very happy that I had called and she was hoping she would hear from me sometime. I told her I was in Reno and that I might be traveling in her direction in the next few days and wanted to know if she would be around. I was trying to sound casual, but I don't know if I did. She said it would be wonderful if I visited and then she asked if I had a place to stay because there was plenty of space on her farm if I wanted. She asked how long I could stay and I didn't really know. I didn't tell her about my troubles although I wanted to. She said she would be very happy to see me when I got there and I should call her when I knew when I would arrive. I said I would. Durinda has a really nice voice. After I hung up Francisco came back to the table and said he needed to get over to the rodeo.

Reno Rodeo ★ ★ ★ ★ ★

This really is my "first rodeo."☺ My friend Francisco got me in for free because he is competing in the calf roping competition with his horse, Sargento. This was especially fun for me because now I had a rooting interest in the competition. I had to leave Sadie in the truck because they don't allow dogs in the rodeo, but it wasn't hot out and she seemed content there with the windows open and some water. Francisco said that he probably wasn't the best calf roper entered today, but he was still pretty good and he had a good chance to win some prize money. I feel bad that I got mad at Francisco last night after he nearly got me in big trouble setting off fireworks, but really I am grateful to him for helping me get to Reno from Bishop, CA, where my car broke down and also for making me get in touch with my friend Durinda. I don't know yet how I will get to Creswell, Oregon, to see her, but now that I have spoken to Durinda who has invited me to come visit her, I am totally determined to find a way. The rodeo is a dirt ring surrounded by bleachers. The bleacher seats were not very comfortable, and the sun was in my eyes for most of it, but the show was really great. I learned that there are seven events in the rodeo—bareback riding, steer wrestling, team roping, saddle bronc, tie-down roping (calf roping), barrel racing and bull riding. Although the events are exciting, I didn't want to see anyone get hurt, especially Francisco. I was able to visit with him in the stables area before things started. Francisco told me that before he starts he is supposed to wait in the "box" while the calf is let out and the judges give him the signal to take off and lasso it. He then jumps off Sargento and wrestles the calf onto its side ("flanking" it) and then with a little rope he carries in his teeth he has to tie three legs of the calf together as fast as he can. The knot is called a "hooey," don't ask me why. The fastest time gets the top prize of $4000. Francisco said that he was hoping to get at least the $1000 third prize so he could pay his expenses. I have to admit that part of me was rooting for the calf, even though Francisco says that the calves who weigh 250 pounds never get hurt, but I have learned not to believe everything Francisco says. Each cowboy gets two tries. The best time of the first three ropers was 10.7 seconds when Francisco was up, but he galloped out of the box too soon and even though he roped and tied up the calf in 10.8 seconds (two raps and a hooey as they say here), the judges gave him a ten-second penalty. He looked pretty unhappy. The second time he got out of the gate fine and the clock said 9.8 seconds when he threw up his arms to show he had finished roping which was by far the best time of anyone, but then the calf broke free from its tie before the six-second waiting period was up, so Francisco was disqualified. After it happened I tried to get over to the area behind the fence where he was, but they wouldn't let me in. I could see him kicking a fence and swearing at himself. I got his attention and he came over and when I said that his 9.8 seconds time before the calf broke free was a great time, he said that he was just a dumb loser and that I should move on. He told me he was going to load up Sargento and go back home as soon as he could get out of there. I said that I needed to get Sadie out of his truck which I knew was the last thing he wanted to hear about, but he went over to the parking lot with me and opened up the truck and got Sadie. I tried to thank him for all he had done for me, but he was in no mood, so I just left. I felt bad.

Greyhound Bus Station (Reno) ★ ★ ★

I am now on my way to Eugene, Oregon, and the town of Creswell to visit my friend Durinda who has invited me to stay for a while. After leaving my friend Francisco at the Reno Rodeo Grounds, a buddy of his offered to take me to the Greyhound station so I could take the bus to Eugene. The bus station was a little run down and there were homeless people sitting or sleeping on some of the benches inside. When I went to the ticket window the woman behind it wasn't very friendly but she told me a ticket to Eugene would cost $153 and it would take about fifteen hours for the trip by way of Sacramento with a transfer to another bus. That sounded like a long time traveling to go 400 miles and $153 would pretty much take all of the money I had left. When I asked if I could take Sadie on the bus, the woman said that dogs aren't allowed on the bus unless they are service dogs and they don't take dogs in crates as baggage. When I told her we really need to get to Eugene she said I could try at the airport although she wasn't sure if there was service from Reno to Eugene. I did think about an airplane, but there is no way I would put Sadie in a cargo hold of an airplane, especially because I have heard of pets dying and getting lost on airplane flights. Also I am sure my $153 remaining is not enough for airfare for the two of us and also I would hate to arrive to see Durinda in Eugene totally broke. As I was walking out with Sadie I noticed that there was a slot machine in the lobby. They are everywhere in Reno, even at the Players Motel where I stayed last night. I thought maybe I should give it a shot, just to see what would happen, but I also felt like this wasn't a lucky day. It was probably the opposite. I have never played a slot machine, but I have some experience with playing online poker at home in Santa Monica. I don't like to talk about it, because I did get a little too obsessed with it although I did pretty well playing it for a while. Maybe I even got addicted to it. In one all-night session I lost seven hundred dollars that my mother saw on my credit card statement. Even though I explained I hadn't really lost in the long run, I promised her I would never gamble again and I haven't. The odds on a slot machine are very much against you. I read you can get a jackpot on most machines about once in 625 times. By the way, I am not an autistic savant like Rain Man. I am just good at math and understand betting. I did take a dollar and put it in the slot for the heck of it and suddenly some bells rang as two cherries out of five lined up. A simple calculation says this is a one in five chance and I got it first time out. The machine spit out three silver dollars. I took the money and left feeling a little bit better.

Reno 24-Hour On-Call Taxi Service ★ ★ ★ ★ ★

When my dog, Sadie, and I exited the Greyhound bus station in Reno, Nevada, I was in a pickle because I needed to get to Eugene, Oregon, and Greyhound won't allow dogs on their buses, which seems especially dumb as all of their buses have pictures of Greyhound dogs on the side. Before I got to the curb a short, bald man with a scruffy beard driving a yellow taxicab asked if I needed a ride to a casino. He sounded like he had a Russian accent. He probably thought I just came in off a bus to go gambling at the casinos. I was going to say no, but then I asked him how much it would cost for him to take me to Eugene, Oregon. I could see he didn't believe me, but I told him I really need to get there and I can't take a bus or a plane because of my dog. He thought for a moment and said $700. I told him that all I had was $155, which was two dollars more than I had five minutes ago as I had just won $2 in a slot machine inside the station. He laughed that $155 wouldn't even pay for gas for him to go there and drive back. He asked if I wanted a ride to a casino. I said I wasn't sure where I would go right now as I needed to get to Eugene and I didn't know how I would do it.

He said if I go to a casino maybe I could turn the $155 into $700. He said he had a fare two months ago that went into a casino with $50 and walked out with $6000! He said that because the man won over $5000 he had to fill out a tax form and pay taxes, so if I win I should definitely quit before I got to $5000. He told me my best odds were with craps, but I never played craps. It might seem at first to you like a totally dumb idea, but I asked him if they had online poker at the casino because I used to play poker online quite a bit. He said they did, but I would be better off playing table poker because the casino video poker machines are a completely different game and the game at the tables is much closer to online poker. Also he said if I wasn't a good player I would need to be very lucky. I asked how much it would cost for a ride to the casino and he said about $12 and I said I'd take the bus because I was short on money. Then he said he was on his way to the taxi lineup at Neptune Casino anyway, so if I got in right away he'd take me for half price. I said okay and got in the cab. The name on his permit was Yvgeny Olenikov. He reached around to pet Sadie on her head and she licked him in the face which made him smile. He asked if he could give her a piece of turkey out of his sandwich and I said okay. He said the casinos only allow service dogs inside but maybe I could tie her outside but I would never consider leaving Sadie alone on the street. We drove for a minute and then he offered to watch Sadie in the cab for $20 while I was inside. I had never left Sadie with anybody else before. What if he got a fare? Yvgeny said I have his Reno taxi registration number and if he's not in the taxi line when I come out all I have to do is call him and he'll come back as soon as he drops off his fare. I wasn't sure. Then he said he could see I was a gambler (although I did once promise my mother no more online poker) and he was a gambler himself and he'd make me a bet. If I lost in the Neptune I would pay him nothing, but if I won I'd give him $40. I hated to trust Sadie to him, but she did seem to like him and she probably has better sense about people than I do. When we stopped at the front entrance to the Neptune, I can't say I wasn't pretty nervous about the whole deal.

Neptune Casino Reno ★★★

When I walked in all I saw was rows of clanging slot machines that filled a big room that smelled of cigarette smoke. No more smoke-free California! I was on a mission to play poker to make enough money to get me to Oregon so I made my way through to the poker room in the back. I have never played live casino poker before and this could be a really dumb idea. There were about six tables in the room and three of them were being played on. I stood behind one of the tables with seven or eight people sitting and watched for a few minutes. It was a big relief that the game seemed pretty much the same as online although having to play with other live, breathing players complicates it for me. They were playing mostly with white and red chips—$1 and $5. I had already made a plan to limit myself to $100 and not go over that because I only had $149 left, enough for a few meals if I lost. There was an empty seat at the second table and, when I approached, the older man sitting on the right moved over to make room. That meant of course I had to sit down. When he turned to me I saw he was wearing a T-shirt with a picture of a Waco biplane on it, one of my favorite classic planes, and underneath it said "I'm not better than you, just way cooler." He had a big stack of chips in front of him, maybe $700 or $800 worth. Wow! Trying to act like this happened every day, I pulled five twenties out of my wallet and handed them to the dealer and she gave me 100 white $1 chips in a little rack and stuffed my bills down a slot. My first strategy was to fold immediately on the first orbit (if you aren't a poker player it means once around the table) unless I somehow got dealt a really strong hand. After I got the rhythm, I made a few small bets but still folded early. Including the blinds, I was only down $16, waiting for something better. The man with the airplane shirt next to me whispered that I should be careful about showing my hand. I am used to playing online and forgot to hide my cards. I said I like his shirt and that the Waco, particularly the YMF5 open cockpit trainer on his shirt, was one of my all-time favorite planes. He said that it was one of his favorites, too and that in fact he owned one in a hangar at Reno Airport. I actually have the Waco YMF5 download for Flight Simulator on my computer! A few hands later, trying hard to be patient and cautious as I couldn't afford a mistake, I turned my cards and then there they were—two beautiful, wonderful kings. I raised to $10. A man in a baseball cap two seats down re-raised to $45. Maybe he was bluffing or maybe not, but odds were he wasn't holding two aces. I went all-in. It was a bold move, but I was thinking that nobody at the table would have taken me for a bluffer, so maybe they would all fold. And then the baseball cap guy just stared at me for what seemed like forever. I mean he just stared. I suppose he was trying to make me break somehow. I did everything I could not to move or breathe. Anyway, he then made kind of a smirk and folded. And just like that I was up $50! Cool! Things were going better than I expected. I folded right away for the next two hands and then it was my turn to be in the big blind and it folded to the man in the Waco shirt who was next to me in the small blind. He raised to $10. I had two eights and I called because I was very aware I had a 12% chance of getting a third eight. The dealer set out a three, a jack and an eight and there it was—a set! I was excited but I tried not to show it. The Waco shirt man bet $25 and I was afraid I couldn't keep a game face on forever, so I raised to $100 to try to end it. He had a big stack but he hadn't been winning that much. He had been playing a bunch of not-that-great hands, maybe because he wanted to stay in the action. He waited for about 2 seconds and then went all-in! If I wanted to get to Oregon, all I could do was to call. My throat was dry and then my leg started doing the sewing machine but I said "call." He said "set, huh?" while nodding and turning over his nine and ten of spades. I was getting really nervous because the Jack and the eight are already out. The next card was a five of diamonds. Nor problem for me. But then he turned over the last river card and it was a queen. He had a straight and beat my three eights. I had lost it all. He collected his $475 pot. It seems like kind of a blur what happened then, but I know that somehow Sadie was the first thing I thought about after the money. I must have run through the casino right out to the taxi line in the front. When I got out front I couldn't find Yvgeny or his taxi or Sadie. I asked the valet and he didn't know. If I lost Sadie then truly I lost everything! Desperate, I searched for Yvgeny's card and I found it in my wallet. I called his number and got voicemail. I texted him. "Where are you? Is Sadie okay?" I had a death grip on my phone while I waited, pacing crazily and I felt everyone was looking at me. I was about to call him again when my phone buzzed with a text. "At airport. Sadie fine. See you 15 mins. Did you win?" I decided to go inside.

Café Al Fresco (Reno) ★ ★ ★ ★

Café of tears! This is the little café near the front of the Neptune Hotel/Casino. I came in here really angry with myself and there must have been tears in my eyes. I had just had an awful experience, foolishly losing almost all the money that I needed to get to Oregon in a poker game. A waitress stopped and looked at me. I thought maybe she might ask me to leave, but instead she asked if I was alright and I said I could use a glass of water because, on top of everything else, I had forgotten to take my medication, another big mistake on my part. I said I was sorry but I didn't need to order anything (I didn't want to spend a precious two dollars on a soda) but she said it would be okay and I could sit at the counter for a bit if I liked. I had fifteen minutes until I hoped I would be reunited with

Sadie, so I sat down at a stool from where I could see the taxi stand. She brought me a glass of water and I took my pill. As I sat there, trying my mental exercises that Dr. DeSantis taught me, the man with the Waco airplane T-shirt who had just beaten me in poker walked in and came up to me. He said that I left so suddenly that he was worried if I was alright. I said that I would be okay, but right now I was mostly thinking about getting my dog back. Then he surprised me. He asked me right out if I was on the spectrum. Nobody ever does that and I was surprised and also kind of relieved that he was so straightforward. Before I could reply he said he has a niece who is autistic and that she is his favorite niece. I told him that my therapist says I have Asperger's although others have said I was high functioning autistic. He said he was sorry for taking my money. I said he didn't take it, he won it and it was fair. He told me his name was Roger. Then he asked how I knew about Waco airplanes because earlier I recognized the one that was printed on his shirt. I explained about how I am an aviation fanatic and I volunteer at the Museum of Flying where they have a restored 1927 Waco model 10 three-seat open cockpit biplane on display. The Waco and their Lockheed Vega are my two favorite vintage planes. He said that he is a pilot and an aviation buff and had owned a few Wacos, but his YMF was definitely his favorite. The YMF is a classic, two-cockpit biplane trainer with a big Continental radial engine that was first built in the 1930s. I can't believe he actually owns one! There is a company in Ohio that was making reproductions. He said that he had a reproduction model for his small air service because his passengers feel safer in a newer plane although it is almost identical to the original plane. He asked if I'd like to take a look at it and I said I would, but I was mostly still thinking about my dog, Sadie, who was supposed to arrive in front in a taxi any minute and I said I would have to go out and look for them.

Reno 24-Hour On-Call TAXI Service ★★★★★

This is my updated review on Reno 24-Hour On-Call Taxi
Service because I used their service twice today and it was more
than excellent both times. Previously Yvgeny Olenikov, the
taxi driver, had done me the favor of watching my dog, Sadie,
while at the Neptune Casino in Reno I stupidly tried to gamble
my way out of a financial problem. Roger, the player who had
beat me fairly in the final poker hand offered to show me his
replica Waco classic airplane at Reno airport. I know he was
trying to make me feel better, although that was hard to do
considering the circumstances. First I had to get my dog, Sadie,
from Yvgeny who met me in front of the Neptune, where Sadie
was really happy to see me, jumping up and down, wagging
her tail wildly and licking my face. Yvgeny wanted to know if
I won or lost in my poker game. I had to tell him I lost, which
disappointed him because he said before that if I lost I wouldn't
have to pay him for watching Sadie. I did open my wallet and
tried to give him $5 but he refused and said that he and Sadie
had become really good friends and that in Reno you never
welsh on a bet. Roger then suggested that we should all take
Yvgeny's cab to the airport to see the Waco. Cool! On the way
to the airport, Roger asked me about myself and I told him my
story of how my mother had died and then my sister tried to
get conservatorship of me but that the court had given it to
Mr. Casabian who was trying to put me in a crummy group
home and drain my bank account. I told him how I ran away
and about my friend Durinda who lives on a farm in Eugene,
Oregon, and how much trouble I have had trying to get there,
as I was unable to take Sadie on a bus or plane. When we got to
the airport he directed Yvgeny to an old hangar in a far corner
of the field that had the names of several aviation companies
painted on the big barn doors. One was "Aero Classics Flight
School, Flight Training, Aerobatics, Sightseeing" and under that
was his name "Roger Wiseman." Roger, Sadie and I got out of

the taxi and said goodbye to Yvgeny. When he paid Yvgeny for the ride I think he gave him a big tip. I hope so. Then he asked me how I would like him to fly the Waco to Eugene! OMG! He said that it might not be too comfortable in the Waco's open cockpit for a long trip, but he could lend me a warm jacket. Yes! Yes! Yes! Roger said that although he has IFR, he'd doesn't like to fly the open cockpit Waco in the dark and, if it was okay with me, we could camp out at his office at the airport until morning. Also that would give him time to check out the plane properly and gas up.

Aero Classics Flight School ★ ★ ★ ★ ★

I was at the Reno airport because Roger Wiseman generously said that he would fly me and my dog, Sadie, to Eugene, Oregon, in his 1934 Waco YMF5 biplane to visit my friend Durinda in Creswell, Oregon. Yesterday, after our cab dropped us off, we went into the hangar through the side doors. I saw the Waco replica on the hangar floor right away among the Pipers and Cessnas. It was painted a very cool electric blue. It was just beautiful in blue. It is just like the original with two open cockpits, one single seat in the back for the pilot (better weight distribution) and a double seat with its own controls in the front for the passenger or trainee—or for me and Sadie, but it had all new instruments and modern avionics. It would be my dream to take the stick, just like I do in Flight Simulator where I use a Thrustmaster Warthog Flight Stick on my computer desk. Roger led me back to his office which was two rooms of plywood walls in the back of the hangar. He went into a cabinet, pulled out a sleeping bag, a mat and a pillow and handed them to me. He said we should leave close to dawn since Creswell (the airport is in nearby Eugene) was about six hours of flying plus a stopover for fuel. He said he would sleep on the couch. Sadie curled up with me on the mat and before I knew it Roger was shaking my shoulder and telling me it was time to get up.

The sun was just coming up. He gave me a down jacket to wear as it would be cold in the open cockpit. Roger showed me how to apply pressure only to the landing gear struts as we pushed the plane out of the hangar. On the tarmac it was incredible to hear the seven-cylinder radial engine roar to life and then I followed Roger in the Waco over to the gas pump for the fill-up for the trip (we would have to refuel half way in Klamath Falls, Oregon). At the gas pump he let me attach the ground wire to the plane and then he pulled out the fuel hose and filled both tanks. I told Roger I would pay him for the gas if I ever got some money, but he said not to worry about it and that he has been wanting for some time to give the Waco a real workout. Then he showed me how to climb into the front cockpit without damaging the skin, strapped me in and handed Sadie to me. I tied Sadie's leash onto my seat harness while Roger climbed into the back, started up the big engine again and we headed down the apron to the runway. Because I have spent so much time at the Santa Monica airport as a docent at the Museum of Flying, I have had the chance to fly in a Cessna Skycatcher, a Cessna 180 (twice), and a De Havilland Beaver. But the Waco is my first ever open cockpit plane and my first classic biplane and my first plane that is certified for aerobatics, although I don't expect we will do any of that. We had to wait at the end of the runway for two planes to land and then Roger got the okay from the tower. The big radial engine thundered and the Waco began to roll. It took more runway than the De Havilland Beaver, but we were lifted off pretty quick and started climbing above Reno. The open cockpit was like being in my dad's old Morgan sports car on the freeway with the top down. When Roger dipped right to make a turn north, I could see Reno and the desert beyond on one side and when he straightened I could see Lake Tahoe on the left. At first Sadie was scared of what was happening and buried her head in my lap, but then I held her so she could look out and feel the wind and she began to get used to it and she stuck her head up. If this was an adventure for me, it had to be a bigger adventure for her. I must say that while I have never had official flying instruction at Aero Classics, based on my experience so far with owner, Roger Wiseman, I totally recommend Aero Classics to anyone.

Crater Lake—Klamath Falls Regional Airport ★ ★ ★ ★ ★

Today, my new friend, Roger, and I flew from Reno in his Waco biplane to Klamath Falls which is halfway to my destination of Eugene, Oregon. It is 355 air miles between Reno and Eugene, but Roger said to be safe we needed to stop to refuel as the Waco has a 375-mile range and if we had a headwind we could easily run out of gas. Also, Roger said that he doesn't like to pee in a bottle, so Klamath Falls would be a good rest stop. This little general aviation airport is very clean and organized with a roomy passenger terminal, not unlike my home airport in Santa Monica. I found water for my dog, Sadie, and Roger and I both used the spotless restroom. Also I bought yogurt and potato chips in the vending machine and they were only a dollar each. I really couldn't find anything to complain about. BUT WAIT!!! HERE IS THE *BIG NEWS*!!! ON THE WAY HERE WE DID A BARREL ROLL IN THE WACO!!! I can't believe it! First off I didn't expect it. When I took off from Reno in Roger's Waco YMF5 biplane on our way to Eugene, Oregon, I was aware the Waco is certified for aerobatics and I knew that Roger was a licensed flight instructor with aerobatic experience, but I also told him when we started that I was a little worried about getting airsick. I expected we would have a simple, smooth flight, since we would have good weather all the way. We passed over the Sierras and I held Sadie up so she could see the snow on Mount Shasta as we approached Klamath Falls. It was getting cold up there, even though there was heat from the big radial engine that came into the cockpit, and I bundled up in the down jacket that Roger lent me. After we left and were in the air for about an hour we were at 4800 feet, traveling at 102 knots and the outside temperature was 44 degrees with Mount Lassen off to the West. Roger spoke to me through my headset and asked if I'd like to try the controls. I had flown the Waco on a flight simulator on my computer at home many times, but being in the real plane was just a different universe. Although I really wanted to just say yes, I said that I didn't want to make some mistake and maybe crash his plane. He told me to try the copilot stick and the rudder pedals to get a feel for them and to try to keep it level and he would keep a loose hand on the pilot's stick in his cockpit. He said not to pay too much attention to the panel kit and more attention to the engine cowling and the horizon and to try to use a light touch, but also to remember we were trying to maintain a compass course of about 310 degrees to get to Klamath Falls. After about ten minutes and a few small corrections from him, Roger pretty much let me have the stick to myself, although it was comforting to know he was there. Then he asked me if I was ready to pilot my first barrel roll. Of course I thought this was a joke, but Roger told me to just keep my hand loose on the stick and he'd do all the work. I said I was worried I would get airsick. I know that in a real barrel roll you will be flying upside down for a few seconds, but I also know that when the maneuver is done correctly you are kept in your seat with one "g" of centrifugal force. Roger said I would barely feel it and he promised I wouldn't get sick and afterwards I could tell the world that I had flown a barrel roll. He didn't wait for me to agree. He just ordered me to keep my hand on the stick so I understood the maneuver and then he gave the Waco a bit of throttle, pulled way back on the stick and then, when we were vertical, pulled the stick hard to the right. I had my hand on the stick, but to be strictly honest, I wasn't the one who was really controlling the airplane. Next thing I knew the trees on the ground were directly over my head. It was all over in about ten seconds. I felt better than fine and Roger said congratulations because now I had done my first barrel roll! Sadie seemed to take it all in her stride, probably because, like everything else this day, it was all new. Later Roger gently brought us into the Klamath Falls Airport, setting us down without a bounce. Now that we were just a few hours away from Eugene, I realized that I hadn't told Durinda exactly when I was coming. I decided I had to phone her. That sounds easy, but in fact it is difficult for me, probably because I am a bit shy. I waited to call her until the last minute before we had to leave, having eaten my snacks and let Roger refuel the Waco and then I finally dialed her number. I got her voicemail and it wasn't even Durinda's voice, just Verizon's automated voice with her phone number asking to leave a message. I left a message saying that I was in Klamath Falls and would be arriving at the Mahlon Sweet Airport in Eugene at approximately 2:00 p.m. I knew that because it was 142 air miles to Eugene and we cruise at approximately 105knots (121 MPH) and we would be taking off a half hour from then at approximately 12:30 p.m. I asked her to please text or leave a voicemail because I needed to know where her farm was. I wasn't sure exactly how I would get to the farm from the airport, but I hoped it wouldn't be too far and I could walk or take a bus. I shouldn't have waited so long to get in touch. I hoped she got my message.

Mahlon Sweet Field ★ ★ ★ ★ ★

My friend, Roger Wiseman, who flew me and my dog, Sadie, to this small general/commercial airport in his Waco biplane from Reno said that most people just call this Eugene Airport, but its real name, Mahlon Sweet, sounds so much better. I found out it is named for an early Oregon automobile dealer and aviator named Mahlon Sweet who organized the first Oregon airshow here in 1919. "Mahlon" reminds me of the Hawaiian word Maholo which means "thank you" and "sweet" just means sweet, so this is like "Thank You Sweet Airport" which is kind of how I feel after finally arriving here. The terminal was fairly new and the tarmac was smooth with the grass nicely cut on the edges and everything spic and span. Roger taxied the Waco over to the fueling area and shut it down. He had already told me that he wanted to gas up again right away to get back home before dark, so I knew it was time to say goodbye to him. When Sadie and I got out and I put on my backpack he put out his arms for me to give him a hug. I'm not a hugger, but in this case it was the least I could do. I told him if I ever got my trust fund back I'd pay him for the gas. I'm not even sure he really believes that I really have a trust fund, but I will pay him back if I can. I turned on my phone and checked to see if I had a message from Durinda while Sadie and I walked over to the general aviation terminal. There was no message and I thought about what I might do and decided I would try Googling for a group community in Eugene or neighboring Creswell. Inside the terminal was a small bank of chairs and I sat down, but then an airport policeman came up to me and said that dogs weren't allowed in the terminal and that I would have to go outside. As I started to leave he asked me why I was in the terminal. I told him the truth, that I had just arrived in a private airplane and I was trying to locate a friend in Eugene. I am not sure if I was nervous because he was looking at me suspiciously or if he was looking at me suspiciously because I was nervous, but I really didn't want to have to answer questions and I especially didn't want to have to show him ID because unfortunately I am still a fugitive with a warrant out for me. Then he asked me what my friend's name was. I hesitated because I didn't want to implicate Durinda in my problems. I knew I had to answer him, but I got stuck and I don't think that he liked that I was taking so long to answer when suddenly I heard my name being called out really loud. "Marcus!!!" I turned around and there was Durinda! She said she got my voicemail and came to meet me, but first went to the wrong terminal! She seemed really happy and excited to see me and that made me feel good and I tried to show her the same thing back. Meanwhile even Sadie got excited and she started barking. When the guard saw that there was someone to greet me he said he hoped we have a good day and he walked away. That left Durinda and me standing there, just kind of looking at each other. Durinda made a funny little laugh and then she put her hand out onto my shoulder and kind of rubbed it a little while she giggled. Then she pulled it back, I think not sure if it was all right to touch me. That was pretty brave of her. She asked me if I had any luggage, but all I had was my backpack. Then she said she had a surprise and she led me outside to the parking lot. Parked right in front of the terminal was a white van with a sign on the side that said "High Meadow Farm—Organic Fruits and Vegetables." There were five people lined up in front of the van. Two of the people were holding hand-written signs. One sign said "Welcome Marcus!!!" and the other said "High Meadow Farm!!" with hearts drawn all around it. I didn't know what to think. Then they all clapped and yelled out my name. It was pretty overwhelming and I'm not sure that I reacted exactly as I should have. I probably should have clapped, back, but I pretty much just stood there in a daze. Then Durinda introduced all of them to me—Donna, Sylvan, Tiffany, and Roberta, I could tell right away that Donna and Sylvan were on the spectrum, too, and probably Tiffany and Roberta, so I guessed they understood how uncomfortable I felt and they didn't seem to mind if I didn't react in a neurotypical way. Tiffany really took to Sadie and she was petting her. Sadie flipped right onto her back and showed Tiffany her tummy for a rub which is a sign that she really liked Tiffany back. Then everybody got in the van with Durinda driving and me in the front passenger seat. That was so cool. I will never forget it!

Prince Puckler's Gourmet Ice Cream
(Eugene, OR) ★ ★ ★ ★ ★

Princes, presidents and butterfat! My friend Durinda took me to
Prince Puckler's Gourmet Ice Cream saying it absolutely had to
be my first Yelp review in Eugene (if you don't count the airport
which is technically on the outskirts of Eugene). When my friend
Durinda came to Los Angeles she said I need to visit her and try
Prince Puckler's but I never thought I would. Durinda, along
with Donna, Sylvan, Tiffany and Roberta had just picked me up
at the airport in Eugene, Oregon, where they were going to take
me back to the group home named High Meadow Farm where
they all live just outside of Eugene. Except they don't call it a
group home. They call it an "intentional community." Donna,
who is the most talkative of the group explained that it's kind
of like what the hippies used to call a commune. Everybody
who lives there has to help run the farm and they share all of
the tasks like cooking and cleaning. It was started by a woman
named Abbie Farnham who, when she was young in the 1960s,
lived on a real hippie commune in California and later had
an autistic son. With the help of an endowment she got from
some rich friends they have kept it going for nine years. It's a
place specifically for high functioning people on the spectrum.
Durinda said that when she told her friends that she was going
to run to the airport to get me, they all wanted to come along.
They wanted to meet me because apparently my Yelp reviews
have made me a minor celebrity in the Aspie world, but also
because they knew if Durinda was driving into town they could
all stop at Prince Puckler's Gourmet Ice Cream. Apparently
everybody in Eugene is very proud of the fact that president
Obama had a mint chip ice cream cone there in 2008 because both
Donna and Tiffany told me about it before we ever got there and
there is a picture inside of him holding up a cone. Durinda said
that Prince Puckler's is near the University of Oregon where
she works part time as a lab assistant. She said that she would

like to show me where she works sometime and I told her that sounded good. Everyone seemed to forget that Sadie and I had just spent the last six hours flying in an open cockpit biplane and I was really overstimulated and tired. I tried my best to not show it because I wanted people to like me, especially Durinda. When it was my turn at the counter, even though everybody told me that I should get Oregon Bing cherry, I first sampled tiger stripes, Muddy River, velvet hammer and chocolate. I also always like to try the regular chocolate because even if I expect to buy a fancy, combination flavor, chocolate is the benchmark for a quality ice cream. I let the chocolate sample linger on my tongue and it was very rich and good, with a strong but slightly fruity chocolate flavor, different but every bit as good as the Van Leeuwen's that I get back home in Santa Monica. Then, for the sake of variety I got a double scoop with Bing cherry and Muddy River, which has brownie batter ice cream with butter fudge ribbon, chocolate truffles and white chocolate flakes inside. The ice cream was especially creamy and I know it had lots of butterfat. The cherry bits tasted like real, fresh cherries. After I finished, Durinda wanted to know how many stars I would give it and I said "maybe two" but I was only joking and everybody knew it and laughed. After that we all got back in the van with me riding shotgun but Tiffany asked if Sadie could sit in her lap and Sadie seemed willing.

High Meadow Farm ★ ★ ★ ★ ★

I gave five stars to High Meadow Farm, but please keep in mind I am still swooning from a great first impression and I reserve the right to revise it later. I have been learning the hard way that everything is not necessarily as it first appears. As I have mentioned in a different review, High Meadow Farm is an "intentional community" set up mostly for people with fairly high functioning autism. It is in Creswell, which is a farming community a few miles south of the city of Eugene in the scenic Willamette Valley. It was started in 2008 by Abbie Farnham and her husband as a safe place for people on the spectrum who may be smart and capable, but also find it hard to navigate the neurotypical world. I arrived here today because my Yelp friend, Durinda (she is Yelp Elite which I hope to be someday), invited me to visit her here. Durinda picked me up when I arrived at the airport in Eugene and, after stopping for ice cream, we drove to a place in the hills outside of town where it is very green and beautiful and then up a long driveway to a farm like you would see in a story book. There is a main farmhouse which is painted white with green trim. It is pretty large with some rambling wings added on and a hundred yards behind it is a big red barn with a round silo and a bunch of other buildings scattered on the property. On a little green hill there is a teepee and two yurts (round, sturdy tents like the ones that nomads in Mongolia use). We parked in front of the farmhouse and right away I saw chickens walking around in the front yard. That really got the attention of my dog, Sadie, who I am pretty sure had never seen a chicken. Fortunately I had her on her leash but she barked and lunged a couple of times and I had to tell her to stop. Durinda brought us inside to the kitchen where I met Abbie Farnham, who looks like she is in her sixties, with gray hair pulled back in a ponytail, wearing jeans and a plaid shirt. She had a big, warm smile and she acted like she already knew me. She petted Sadie who responded by showing her tummy right away. Abbie offered me lemonade and pumpkin bread and we sat at the table and talked. She said that Durinda had told her about me but she wanted to know more about my situation. I was excited but tired and didn't feel like talking all that much, but she kept asking me questions so I wound up telling her the whole story starting with my mother dying, and how the court appointed a conservator and how I ran away when Mr. Casabian, my conservator, tried to put me in a group home and take Sadie away. I left out the part of my story about the warrant that says I supposedly committed a hit and run with my car I think because I was embarrassed and also I didn't want to make her nervous. She told me that she has heard a number of stories like mine and that dividing an estate can definitely bring out the worst in families. She said that I could stay at the farm for a bit while I tried to work things out and that she would try to help me if she could. She said from what she could tell about me so far I probably didn't need an outside conservator if I didn't want one. She said that the farm wasn't accepting any new residents right then but I could stay in the visitor's yurt for the time being and I might like to take part in some of the work and activities there to keep myself busy. She explained that High Meadow Farm is a CSA (Community Supported Agriculture) farm and that people in the area subscribe to receive their organic fruits, vegetables and eggs. That way they don't have to worry too much about selling what they produce, although they still sell at a booth at the farmers' market in town. Only some of the residents work full time on the farm. Some, like Durinda, have other jobs, and a few even have their own small businesses, but everybody has to work on the farm at least fifteen hours a week. Abbie said that I reminded her a lot of her son, Josh, who she said is high functioning autistic and worked at the farm for five years. But she is proud that he is now working on an apple farm in Washington State where he is an expert on breeding and cultivating apples. According to her, Abbie and her husband, Matt, were inspired to start High Meadow Farm by Josh's interest in farming. I have worked at a library and at a museum but I would like to contribute my share while I am here. Then Abbie came with me and Durinda to show me the yurt where I could stay for the "time being." It is next to a field that is planted with beets, kale and carrots. Even though it is really just a sturdy, round tent, it is surprisingly comfortable inside, with a planked wood floor, a big, comfortable bed with a home-made quilt on it, an old dresser painted bright blue and an old lounge chair. Abbie said I must be tired from my trip and they would leave me to get settled. She invited me to dinner later. Durinda said that she had to help with dinner, so I put out the few things I had in my backpack and found the semi-outdoor shower behind the barn. The only problem was that I didn't have any clean clothes to put on, because I only had the few things that I had bought at Walmart a few days ago. So much has happened and it feels like I left a year ago. Durinda told me that they eat early because everyone on a farm goes to bed early and gets up early. There is a huge old wooden table that seats about twenty people in a big room off the kitchen in the main farmhouse and there were eleven people at the table tonight. Tiffany and Sylvan, whom I met at the airport, were there and several others including Abbie and her husband, Matt, who I learned is a construction contractor. We had linguini with peppers and broccoli, an Indian dish with lentils that I didn't know the name of, home-baked rosemary bread and loganberry shortcake for dessert that was made by one of the residents named Josie. Delicious! They cook nearly entirely with food that they grow. Almost everybody is vegetarian or vegan but there are no rules against meat except to cook it in designated pans. Everybody at the table seems to get along very well although, as you would expect from a table full of Aspies, conversation was pretty disjointed. While we were finishing dessert, Jeff, one of the residents, pulled out a guitar and started playing really pretty music that he said was Bach. Durinda told everybody I have a nice singing voice, but I said I really didn't want to sing now and thankfully people seemed to respect that. I am very excited just to be someplace settled and peaceful and not on the run, at least for the moment.

Cottage Laundromat ★ ★ ★ ★

After dinner at the main house at High Meadow Farm where I am staying right now, I went back to my yurt where I sleep. I have had a big day of travel and I was planning on going right to bed, but Durinda came to my door with a big old sofa cushion that she said would be good for Sadie to sleep on. Sadie sniffed at it for a second and then walked around it and then settled her butt into it with a groan. Then Durinda asked if I had enough clean clothes. She probably noticed I put on sweaty clothes after showering. Durinda said we should go to the laundromat in Cottage Grove a few miles down the road. She said she had some laundry to do as well and nobody uses the washing machine in the main house after seven o'clock so as not to disturb the other residents. Even though I was so tired I thought I could drop right then, I really wanted to see more of Durinda and I also wanted clean clothes. I waited outside the main house while Durinda went to her room upstairs and came back with a pillowcase full of laundry and then she drove with me in her white Toyota Corolla about five miles to the laundromat. Cottage Laundromat was in a mini-mall next to a liquor store and was well kept and clean with about a dozen Whirlpool washers. I asked Durinda if she had ever reviewed Cottage Laundromat and she said "Of course. I have reviewed everything that anybody could ever review within ten miles of Creswell." That made me laugh. I asked her to show me her laundromat review on her phone, but she said she would be embarrassed. I had already read most of her 415 reviews, mostly about restaurants in Eugene and Portland, but I didn't remember reading about Cottage Laundromat. She asked if I was planning to review the laundromat and I said "Of course!" and then she laughed. I need all the reviews I can do if I am ever going to make Elite. In fact, Durinda said that she noticed that I hadn't made any reviews lately although she completely understood how busy I was being a fugitive. I told her that I have been writing reviews and saving them in my phone, but not submitting them right now because I shouldn't give my conservator, Robert Casabian, any clues about where I am. This naturally puts my wish of becoming Yelp Elite on hold. (If you are ever reading this online on Yelp now, you will know that at least this part of my life has been settled.) Durinda put her clothes in a washer and said it would be okay if I put my clothes in with hers because I only had a few shirts and underpants and a pair of pants. I am kind of germaphobic and it was enough of a stretch to use a public washing machine without mixing someone else's clothes with mine, even if they were Durinda's, even though I am sure she is an extremely clean person. Also I only wash with hot water, even though it is not supposed to be good for colored clothes and I didn't want to have to ask her if we could choose hot water. I told her that I would be willing to share a dryer, however, and that was okay with her. That's when Durinda said that if we ever got married we would always have our clothes tumbling together. I guess I should have said something, but I didn't know what to say, so I said I was going to just go out in the parking lot for a minute which I did. I really, really like Durinda, but I am finding that being around her also makes me nervous. I did go back inside and we talked some more like nothing had happened. We talked about Yelp a lot. I told her about how mad I was at Barrington Farms for playing Herb Alpert trumpet music, but I still gave it two stars because I didn't want to be like Rambo mean. Now it doesn't seem so important in the light of all the other problems I have. She said that she gives more five stars than anything because she wants to reward businesses that try hard. I think that is a good attitude, too. She said she once gave a one-star review to a Chinese restaurant in Eugene because she saw them slicing raw chicken on the same chopping board as vegetables and she felt that could make people sick. She said she would really like to take me sometime to her favorite five-star places, or it would be fun to review a place in Eugene or Portland that neither of us had been to. The washing machine worked just fine and the dryer only took six quarters to dry all our clothes which is pretty good. When we finished we were the only people in there. On the way back Durinda said that she was sorry if she upset me when she tried to kiss me (which she did when we first met in Los Angeles) and that it would be all right if we were just friends.

Ronan Weber Custom Audio ★ ★ ★ ★ ★

To be honest, I don't have a lot of knowledge (really *any* knowledge) about custom audio, specifically repairing and modifying old German microphones, but I am really impressed by Ronan (no relation to one of my favorite comic book heroes — Ronan the Accuser) Weber. After arriving at High Meadow Farm, an intentional community, where my friend Durinda introduced me to some of the residents and to its founder, Abbie Farnham, I am temporarily staying in a canvas yurt next to a vegetable field. There is no running water inside. I use a "composting toilet" which is in a little outhouse about fifty yards away and shared by the other yurt and a ramshackle old cottage. It is surprisingly clean and doesn't even smell. Late last night (2 a.m.), when I was making a trip to the outhouse I passed by the cottage and lights were on inside. When I walked back to my yurt a young man, perhaps a few years older than me, was standing in front of the cottage drinking Coke from a can and he called out to me, asking if I could help him out for a minute. On the way in he said that some people on the farm think it's bad he drinks so many sugar sodas but he doesn't care what they think. Inside, everything except his bed was electronic testing equipment and bins full of electronic parts, all OCD clean and neatly put away with printed labels on little drawers and shelves. On the workbench was one of those fat, cold-capsule-shaped microphones like you see in a recording studio. Then he handed me a card with something written on it and asked me if I would read something into the microphone and make sure I accentuate the "s" sounds. He said it was from Shakespeare. "Sit down awhile and let us once again assail your ears that are so fortified against our story what we have two nights seen." He didn't tell me why, but I read it anyway while he looked at the graph patterns the sound created on his computer screen. He then explained that he has a mail order business repairing and upgrading classic old German microphones and that recording studios from around the country send him microphones to rebuild and modify. He told me that Harry Connick Junior used a mike he had personally modified. I read what he asked and he said thank you. The Shakespeare was a test to see how the microphone responded to sibilant "S" sounds which is one of the hardest sounds to capture right. Then he said he heard that I got stuck in some kind of bad conservatorship and he thought it was too bad that I couldn't get "SDM" like him after he left home. I didn't know what SDM was so I asked him and he said it was "supported decision making." He said it all started when he told his parents he wanted to move out of their home because they were treating him like a child. He said he knows sometimes he makes dumb decisions, but now he has a team of three "advisors" that he chose himself that support and give him advice on the big things like where to live or how to expand his business or getting good medical care or things like that. They are the ones that got him into High Meadow Farm and they helped him start his business and invest his money. I asked him if his advisors could force him into a group home if they wanted and he said no way. That sounded cool, but it's too late for me, I guess. Then he said everybody on the farm was talking about how Durinda was in love with me. I asked him how he knew that and he said he just "knew." Then he asked if we had "done it." Of course we hadn't and if we had I wouldn't tell him. He said that I should know that the official policy of the farm was that we were adults and could have sex whenever we want and it was none of their business as long as nobody was pressured or harmed and nobody did or said anything that was inappropriate. Of course the problem is that if you are on the spectrum you are always doing something that is inappropriate. Being inappropriate is even the reason that Ronan asked the question. Anyway, I wish I could have "SDM" like Ronan.

Open Space Farms and Ranch Supplies (Creswell) ★ ★ ★ ★ ★

I came to Open Space Farms and Ranch Supplies with Sylvan in a pickup truck to get things we needed for High Meadow Farm where I am staying. This is all new to me as I am really a city person, but I really like this store. One thing I like about it is finding something I never even knew existed, like last time I was here I saw a 25-ton log splitter that uses a four-stroke gas engine. This time I saw in the back a hand-crank stainless steel tabletop sausage-stuffer. I don't think they sell those in Santa Monica. Outside the store they stack bags of feed and fertilizer, fencing and rolls of screening and inside are things like tools, boots, generators, irrigation parts, chemicals (High Meadow Farm is organic, so we pass on those), seeds and canning jars. Sylvan is the farm manager and probably the person who looks and acts most like a real farmer. He's slim and wears worn blue jeans and Western shirts and knows more about farming than anyone around. I am not sure if he is slightly on the spectrum or maybe he is just kind of quiet by nature. It's not always true when they say "it takes one to know one." We are here mostly to get alfalfa which we will mix in with the kitchen scraps to feed the chickens. Sylvan says that he wishes we didn't have to supplement the kitchen scraps at all to feed the chickens and hopes we can stop doing it soon. He is a great believer in a type of farming they call "Permaculture," that basically means that a farm should be a closed ecological system where the plants and the animals all complement and complete each other in a way that you don't have to kill weeds or insects or trap varmints to keep things going as they all become part of the whole Eco-structure. The farm is already certified organic because it doesn't use any pesticides, but Permaculture is one step beyond organic and even better for the environment. He says it's really hard to do on a farm that has only ten acres but the idea is to just keep going in that direction and that someday the farm could be entirely self-sustaining. I have read several books about farming (I recommend *Permaculture—A Designer's Manual* by Bill Morrison) that I borrowed from the bookshelf in the main house. I have learned a lot since I have been here although there is clearly much more I need to know and it is very challenging. Yesterday I moved tomato seedlings from the greenhouse to outside because unless they are in some wind they won't develop enough cellulose to keep the stalks strong. I stir the compost pile every afternoon and I collect eggs from our chickens twice a day. When I first had to move a hen to get at her egg I felt pretty weird and intrusive, but now I am used to it and the hens don't seem to mind as much as you would expect. When my dog, Sadie, saw her first chicken she barked at it, and later she ran after a hen, but the hen fluttered and attacked her and now she leaves them alone and they leave her alone. Since she is getting along fine with the chickens, I have been able to let her roam the farm off the leash along with the three other dogs on the farm—Shadow, Loki and Daisy. Shadow is a yellow Lab. Loki is a pit bull mix but seems to be a very sweet dog. Daisy is an Australian Shepherd. I didn't know if Sadie would get along with other dogs since she was really more a people dog, but now they all seem to hang out pretty well together and they stay around the house or go off chasing squirrels except for Daisy who is 12 years old and can't move too well. Sadie seems a little less attached to me now that she has friends and can roam off leash, but I suppose that is probably a good thing for Sadie.

All we really needed at the store was a bale of alfalfa, several irrigation connectors and a pack of white marking stakes. At the register, they were selling individual homemade apple pies for three dollars from Sharon Josephson, the wife of the owner, and I bought one for me and one for Sylvan. Although I came to the farm with almost no money after having lost $675 in one poker hand in Reno, Abbie Farnham, who started the farm is now paying me $12 an hour to help build a straw bale house on the property which they will use for future residents so now I don't feel so poor. In case you didn't know, a straw bale house is made by piling big bales of straw for walls that you then plaster over to make it waterproof. It is very well insulated and will be warm in the winter and cool in the summer without heat or air conditioning and it is very cheap and easy to build. I was thinking that maybe I would like to live in it someday, but I shouldn't even think that as right now I am a fugitive because I have a warrant out for me for having fled from my conservator and also for running from an accident (which is a lie).

ZIRC ★★★★★

I bet you are wondering what "ZIRC" is, especially since this is the premier first review on Yelp for ZIRC (I hope the Yelp Elite committee takes note of this). I was wondering, too, until my friend Durinda took me to work with her today. ZIRC stands for Zebrafish International Research Center which is at the University of Oregon in Eugene. I didn't know what a zebrafish was until I met Durinda who knows everything about zebrafish, especially zebrafish husbandry which means breeding. She is really amazing, as is ZIRC. Did you know that 84% of human genes associated with disease are also found in zebrafish? They breed every ten days and produce up to 300 eggs at a time. And their embryos are outside their bodies, which makes them so accessible for scientists to work on. For example, they can model melanoma (a kind of cancer) in a zebrafish and then try to treat the melanoma and see if the treatment works. Also muscular dystrophy. Durinda showed me a bunch of them in a tank here and they look like little striped minnows. The stripes are why they are called zebrafish. Durinda is an expert on how to breed and raise them which is very technical. Scientists have very rigid standards for raising them for use in laboratories. Another good thing is that if you are going to have to experiment on an animal to save human lives, I think it is better to use a fish instead of a mouse. Of course since we don't absolutely know what fish are thinking about being experimented on as opposed to mice, there may be some debate. Durinda said that I would only be able to stay for a few minutes because she didn't want to disturb the work in the facility, but I was very impressed. Everyone seemed happy to see her when she came in. She told me on the way over from Creswell where she lives that they want her to work more than part time, but she says that more than 20 hours would be too much stimulation for her and also she loves the time she spends at High Meadow Farm doing farm work and being with the other residents.

Oregon Air and Space Museum ★ ★ ★ ★ ★

I had no idea there was an actual air museum in Eugene until my new neighbor Ronan told me about it after I mentioned my interest in airplanes. Of course I wanted to check it out ASAP and today I came into Eugene with my friend Durinda who took me to where she works and then lent me her car so that I could visit the museum. She said that I could pick her up in four hours but that, in return, I would have to bring her a cup of Bing cherry ice cream from Prince Puckler's Gourmet Ice Cream. The museum is smaller than the Santa Monica Museum of Flying where I was recently a docent. It is located at the Mahlon Sweet Airport in Eugene just a few hundred yards from where I first landed a few weeks ago on my Oregon adventure. I got here an hour before the museum opened at 10 a.m., but that was okay because I spent some time plane spotting next to the runway where, among other planes, I saw a United Airlines Embraer ER175 and a Cessna Citation X business jet touch down. When I came back to the museum the door was open and there was an older man at the counter at the entrance but nobody had gone into the museum yet. I don't think they have many customers on a weekday. I paid him the $7 admission fee which is less than the $10 we charged at the Museum of Flying. Inside I could see that crammed into a space the size of a high school gym they had several classic airplanes, some of them military including an A4 Skyhawk and a Mig17. The most interesting plane was the 1916 Nieuport fighter which is a sesquiplane. That means that it is a biplane, but the lower wing is much smaller than the upper wing. I asked the man if it had been built in France or Italy. I knew it had once been built in both countries and he said it was French, which is more typical. He said his name was Doug and that I seemed to know a lot about airplanes. I told him that until recently I had been a docent at the Santa Monica Museum of Flying, right where Douglas Airplanes used to be assembled and that my favorite plane was the Douglas DC-3, but I also like classic early biplanes. He asked if I wanted to sit in the Nieuport and of course I jumped at the chance. He said that he once piloted an Air Force F4 in Vietnam, but that he had briefly flown DC-3s in the Caribbean and had great respect for them. We wound up talking about airplanes for a long time and I learned that the North Vietnamese flew little Antonov N2 biplanes for reconnaissance and short deliveries of personnel and equipment, and the Air Force had several De Havilland Beavers (one of my favorite small planes) which the Americans used in the same way as the Antonovs. Then he asked if I was going to be in Eugene for a while and I said that I wasn't certain, but was living on a farm in nearby Creswell. He said that they were in need of docents and wanted to know if I would be interested. That seemed like a very good opportunity, but rather than explain that I was currently a fugitive and it might not be a good idea right now, I told him that I would have to think about it and let him know later. I think that I would enjoy being a docent in this little museum, partly because that would make me a bigger fish in a little pond, if you know what I mean.

Creswell Auto Service ★★★★★

Creswell Auto Service sells gas but has a repair garage as well. The Shell station on the other side of town is a little newer and fancier, and you can buy sandwiches and candy inside, but they can't help you if your car is broken. Everyone at High Meadow Farm buys gas here. Believe it or not the law in Oregon says you aren't allowed to fill up your own gas tank and an attendant has to do it for you which keeps them busy all the time. The owner, Dennis Fraser, knows all of the farm residents by name (including me, although I am not officially a resident), helps to maintain their cars and also helps run the VFW bingo night. He lets my friend Durinda who besides being an expert on zebrafish, is a very good mechanic, use his tools and his lift to work on her car and some of the farm equipment. I think that this is part of the Oregon spirit that I am discovering. Much as I like my native Santa Monica, I don't know of any garage there that would let a customer use their tools. I went along with Durinda when she brought the farm's Kubota tractor to Creswell Auto Service because, according to her, the hydraulic cylinder that controls the steering was leaking which made it dangerous to drive. She had a new cylinder that came the day before by UPS, but she needed some special wrenches to install it. Also, it would be easier if the tractor was up on a lift so she wouldn't have to crawl on her back. She brought Dennis a big box of broccoli and tomatoes from the farm and he thanked her. Durinda has her own mechanic's coveralls with her name and the name of her dad's garage in Portland, *Dowling Tire and Auto,* on the front pocket. That's where she learned to be a mechanic until she decided she could go to college and enrolled at Portland State majoring in biology. When one of the nuts holding the hydraulic cylinder to the tractor frame wouldn't budge even after spraying it with WD40 and using a long handled wrench, Durinda asked Dennis for a blowtorch and then showed me how to heat the nut with a blowtorch to free it. It took about four hours to fix the tractor but I didn't mind because I enjoy being with Durinda and we find lots of things to talk about. For example, I found out that Durinda knows all the words to all the songs in *The Music Man*. I told her that I really like musicals from the Broadway Golden Age in the fifties and sixties. At a spring concert at the First Congregational in Santa Monica my choir sang "Lida Rose" in four-part close harmony. While she was putting in the cylinder we sang "Gary Indiana" together: Durinda's sense of pitch is not nearly as good as mine, but I can't believe she got every word to all the verses. The choir director at the church used to say to some of the parishioners in the regular choir who tried out for the concert choir but got rejected that they "sing with great enthusiasm." That describes Durinda. She asked which *Music Man* song was my favorite and I said "Till There Was You," and she said it was her favorite, too. It's a very romantic song written by Meredith Wilson, the creator of *The Music Man*. He wrote it as a duet and Durinda started singing it and we sang that together, too. When we sang the lyrics I think we were both thinking the same thing, but neither of us was ever going to say what that was. Maybe you know. Dennis Fraser came up from the office and we stopped, but then he asked us to keep singing because he thought it was pretty cute.

Law Office of Samuel Springer ★ ★

Abbie Farnham, who owns High Meadow Farm and is my

friend now, made an appointment in Eugene for me to see Mr. Springer who is an attorney who specializes in what they call "eldercare" and also in guardianships which is the same thing as what they call a conservatorship in California. I was worried about paying him, but Abbie said that she had arranged a one-hour free consult. Mr. Springer had a small office over a shop that sells Belgian Waffles in downtown Eugene and sometime I would like to try the waffles and review them, but not today as Abbie has a busy schedule. Mr. Springer seemed friendly enough, but when I told him my story of being forced into a conservatorship with Mr. Casabian and then running away when he tried to put me in a group home, he had several serious questions about how the court ruled, most of which I was able to answer. I didn't tell him about the warrant I had for hit and run, partly because I hadn't told Abbie and I didn't want to have her find out then. After we talked for a while and he took notes on a yellow pad he took a deep breath and spoke mostly to Abbie and not to me. He said that I was in a very tough spot. He said that although he doesn't practice in California, he knows that under California law it is almost impossible to dissolve a conservatorship once it has been established in the probate court. It would cost thousands of dollars to try in the courts and Mr. Casabian, who holds my purse strings, would never allow me to pay for it. He was afraid that I had been caught in a very bad system that would allow Mr. Casabian, if he chose, to deplete my inheritance by charging me hundreds of dollars an hour fees every time he filled out a legal form or chatted with his attorneys about me. That is common. What's worse is, since there is no good watchdog to keep an eye on them, professional guardians sometimes commit actual fraud to get at your estate. He also said he was sorry but that there wasn't anything he could do for me. He thought that Mr. Casabian would probably find me, using money from my inheritance to hire someone to look for me if necessary, and it would be very hard for me not to wind up in a group home against my will. When Abbie and I left we really didn't say much to each other, but when we got back to High Meadow Farm Abbie said that Mr. Springer's wasn't the only opinion out there and she wasn't ready to give up and she hoped I wasn't. I told her I wasn't, but the whole thing didn't make me feel good.

Creswell VFW Bingo Night ★ ★ ★ ★ ★

I know about bingo night at the VFW because Raoul, the appliance repair man who came to fix the refrigerator in the main house, is in charge of it. I watched him replace the compressor in the farm's big double-door Samsung refrigerator which was pretty interesting by itself and he asked me if I was coming with the other residents to bingo on Friday. He said every second Friday the VFW post in Creswell hosts bingo and everyone has a good time. Considering my current situation of being unable to get rid of my conservator, a good time sounded agreeable. It starts at 6:30 and then there is an 8 p.m. music and pizza break when a group from the high school plays music and they sell slices from Figaro's Pizza for $5 apiece at the bar. Sylvan, the High Meadow Farm manager who everyone agrees is the best night-time driver, always takes a group of seven or eight residents—whoever wants to go. I asked Sylvan and he said there was room in the van, so I went and it was really a fun experience and besides, Durinda said she wanted to go, too. You can get six bingo cards for $5. A dauber costs $2 and you can win up to $250 if you are very lucky. The VFW is in a big old building on the main street in Creswell. It's not just veterans who show up, but it is mostly older, retired people. Raoul, who is the VFW commander when he isn't fixing refrigerators, was calling out the numbers. Most of the vets were from the Vietnam War, some from Desert Storm, and Sylvan said one or two really old guys in army hats were in the Korean War. They sell lemonade next to the pizza, but you can also buy several kinds of beer at the bar in the back which seemed pretty popular with a bunch of the vets. I noticed that Dennis Fraser, from the Creswell Auto Service was sitting on a stool back there with three empty bottles in front of him. I bought $25 worth of cards because that's what most people did, although I was still stinging from having lost all my money playing poker in Reno. Durinda bought $25 worth, too and she said we should join forces and split our winnings which sounded like a good idea. By the time the pizza and music break came along, we had gotten two bingos together and just about broke even. Then Raoul announced that there was no music that night because two of the band members had to study for finals. That's when Dennis Fraser, who was clearly a couple of beers over the line, got up off his stool and announced to Raoul and anyone who would listen that there were two talented singers in the room and if everybody showed some enthusiasm maybe they would sing a few songs for the break. He pointed at us and everybody in the room started clapping and yelling for us to sing. That was pretty embarrassing. It is true, though, that even though I am very shy in small groups, I am not more afraid to get up in front of a hundred people than two people. One of the things I miss most from Santa Monica is performing in the First Congregational Church Choir concerts. I have a good tenor voice and I sing in the concert choir, even though I am Jewish. But I didn't want to make Durinda feel bad. She is a wonderful person, but even though she sings with enthusiasm, singing isn't her talent. If you read this Durinda, I hope you don't take it personally or get mad at me. Anyway, Durinda, instead of being shy, pulled me up onto the stage where there was a microphone and she told everyone how great it was that we both loved *The Music Man* and then a Capella we sang "76 Trombones," "Gary Indiana," "Good Night My Someone," and "Marian the Librarian." Even though we sang pretty off key as a duet, everybody applauded and whistled and one of the vets who was probably even drunker than Dennis shouted for an encore so we sang "Till There Was You." which is a very sweet and romantic love song and I guess that's why Durinda cried after. And then it was time for bingo again. Afterwards everyone congratulated us, even Sylvan and the other High Meadow residents. It was all pretty amazing and in the van on the way home everybody sang or tried to sing "76 Trombones." Actually it is a song I love, but can't listen to from the actual cast album as the noise of the trombones is upsetting to me. When I got back to the farm, Abbie was on the porch waiting for us and asked for me to come inside to talk to her. When I got inside she told me that a Lane County Deputy Sheriff had come to the farm while I was gone and said he was looking for me. She wanted to know why.

Harry Chauncy and AAGA (Americans Against Guardianship Abuse) ★ ★ ★ ★ ★

Abbie Farnham, who runs the High Meadow Farm intentional community drove me to Portland today to meet with Mr. Chauncy, a founding member of a group called Americans Against Guardianship Abuse. He does *pro bono* (no pay) work to help people who are caught in abusive conservatorships. Abbie, who is a very persistent person, found Mr. Chauncy after we had a disappointing meeting with a guardianship attorney in Eugene. Because my conservator, Robert Casabian, has complete control of my finances, I am not allowed to pay my own lawyer to work for my benefit and not his. Someone said it is a "Catch 22," which I know about because the movie *Catch 22* used the largest assembly of original World War II B25 bombers ever put together and I watched it four times. Before we went into his office, Abbie told me that Mr. Chauncy helped start AAGA after his wife's elderly father was forced by the court into a court-appointed conservatorship against his will. The conservator then refused to allow his wife to see her 90-year-old father and took all of his savings in fees leaving him penniless and alone when he died. Abbie thought that Mr. Chauncy might be interested in my case and I am really glad he was. He had an office in downtown Portland. It was a little messy, but I noticed the law degree on his wall was from Yale, so he should be a pretty good lawyer. I noticed right away that part of his jaw had been cut away and scarred, maybe an accident or cancer, which hurt his good looks and his speech was a little slurry. I am sorry that this happened to him, but I think maybe it puts me more at ease to be with someone who might have has his own personal struggles. I told him about how my mother died and how, when my sister and my stepfather both applied for conservatorship, the court appointed a professional conservator instead. Abbie said that she didn't think I really needed a legal conservator, just people to help me with some of the issues I face like the "supported decision making" team my friend Ronan has. Mr. Chauncy said that having a conservator forced on a person with an estate happens too much and that many judges have cozy relationships with conservators and push business their way. I explained that Mr. Casabian tried to stash me in an awful group home in Woodland Hills and take Sadie away from me and that I ran away and am now a fugitive. He wanted to know if there was a warrant out for me. I said that I believed there was a "writ of assistance" because a policeman on the Walker River Indian Reservation had told me so. I foolishly didn't mention the bogus warrant for a hit and run automobile accident. I wish I had because after I told him my story he went on his computer for a few minutes and when he looked back up he asked me if I knew anything about a criminal warrant for a hit and run incident in Woodland Hills. OMG! I was really embarrassed and decided to come clean and admit that the Walker River policeman had mentioned it to me. He didn't seem too bothered but I could see that Abby was looking kind of shocked. I told him that all I knew was that when I started driving off from the parking lot of the group home that Mr. Casabian pounded on the trunk of my car but I am sure I never hit him. If I had injured anyone I certainly would have stopped right away. He said that it was important that I tell him everything honestly or he wouldn't be able to help me. Abbie said that she wished I had told her, too. I felt really bad for not being totally honest before, but I said again that I never hit anybody with my car, and if anything, Robert Casabian had hit me. Abbie asked Mr. Chauncy whether we needed to go to the police now. She said she was worried now that she could somehow be liable for hiding a fugitive and that it could jeopardize High Meadow Farm. I would just hate for that to happen. Mr. Chauncy told her that he couldn't advise her what to do right now, but he said he would look into it and if she could wait just a bit to contact the police, he would try to learn more. He said that a California warrant might not be a high priority for the local police and it could be a few days before they got around to me again. On the drive back home Abbie said that I had let her and the farm down by not telling her about the hit-and-run. I said I was really sorry and I hoped that didn't mean I would have to leave. She said she would wait to hear from Mr. Chauncy, but never to hide anything else from her. I again said how sorry I was for not having told her everything before and that was the truth. I feel really terrible.

Creswell Farmers' Market ★ ★ ★ ★ ★

This turned out to be a big day for me, but let me tell you about the Creswell Farmers' market first and then I'll tell you what happened. Pretty much all of the local small farms as well as several crafts vendors have booths in the library parking lot on Tuesday afternoons. I have gotten to know some of the other exhibitors since I have been helping out in the High Meadow Farm booth for a few weeks now. It is a friendly competition, where one week we may have the best Treasure Trove tomatoes and the next week it may be Louis at Dexter Farms or Jose at

Cottage Farms. Everyone tries to keep the prices fair but not to undercut each other too much. In order to have a booth at the market you have to have grown your produce within forty miles of Creswell. The purses and dishcloths and paintings that they sell in the crafts booth have to be handmade and local. Irena Gonzales who is a few booths down makes really nice quilts and decorated pillowcases. The market is very popular and people come from all around, including Eugene. Sometimes I work at the counter, but today was really busy and we sold out of zucchini and red bell peppers, so Sylvan and I took the van back to the farm to get a few more boxes. Tiffany and Durinda were in charge of the booth, with Durinda handling the cash box because she is very good at numbers and keeping track. When Sylvan and I got back from the farm there was a policeman in uniform at the booth talking to Durinda. I could see she was upset. I was holding a box of zucchini trying to tell what was going on when the policeman saw me and asked me if I was Marcus Katz. Then Durinda asked him to leave me alone. Suddenly I felt this physical feeling like my world was collapsing underneath me—the farm, Durinda, all my friends, Oregon. Everything that I may have once feared but had grown to love. Someone, I'm not sure who, yelled at me to run, but that would have been dumb. The policeman took a step toward me and I just froze. Then suddenly Sylvan stepped between us to talk to the policeman. He asked him what he wanted with me and the policeman said I needed to come to the station with him and Sylvan asked why and the policeman said in a very policeman-like voice that Sylvan shouldn't interfere and Sylvan asked him if I was under arrest and the policeman again said that Sylvan shouldn't interfere. Then Durinda yelled at the policeman that I hadn't done anything and then I started acting panicky. I was rocking and moaning and on my way toward a grade AA meltdown. That's when Durinda told him that he was making me sick and that I had a "condition" and he needed to leave me alone because I wasn't hurting anybody. Meanwhile people started crowding around. The policeman spoke into his radio asking for help. Then Sylvan asked him if he had a warrant for me and the policeman said there was a warrant but he didn't have it with him and that also I was a missing person. Sylvan told him that if I was here I wasn't missing anymore and he should go. The other policeman, a sergeant, arrived and there was beginning to be a crowd. People started holding up their phones in the air to take videos. The sergeant then came toward me trying his best to act totally calm and cool and asked me to come with him to the sheriff's station so we could "straighten things out." Then I saw Dennis Fraser from the Creswell Auto Service come over from another booth and he spoke to the sergeant who he called Henry. He said he wanted to know what the problem was because he said I was a good kid. That's when the sergeant tried to grab me by the shoulder. I naturally resisted, not just because he was a policeman, but because I really, really don't like being grabbed. I backed off a couple of steps quickly and then a weird thing happened. Sylvan, Durinda and Tiffany all managed to put themselves between me and him to protect me and then so did Dennis. Then some other people who happened to be there, some of whom I knew as customers for the farm stand and some whom I recognized from the VFW, and also Merlin and Nicole who run the Peaceable Palate food truck started gathering around me in a circle, protecting me, yelling for the policemen to leave me alone and not to touch me. Meanwhile all the phone cameras were obviously making the police nervous and it was kind of a standoff. But even in my panic I knew there was no place to run and I especially didn't want to run from Creswell and the farm and Durinda. I told the sergeant that if he didn't grab me or try to put me in handcuffs that I would come with him to the police station and then I walked with them to the police car and got in. I could see Durinda dial her phone to call Abbie. Fortunately

I didn't have the whole meltdown. I don't know why. Maybe because of all the good, organic food from the farm I have been eating.

Lane County Sheriff Creswell Substation ★ ★ ★

I am not sure how you rate a police station. I can say the paint on the wall is fresh and the chairs are uncomfortable but that doesn't really describe it. Despite a misunderstanding I had with the two policemen who arrested me, the police here have been polite and businesslike. I have two warrants from California. This is what the detective sergeant said to me after I was brought in a police car from my job at the Creswell Farmers' market to the Creswell Sheriff's substation. The first is technically something called a "writ of assistance" for being a runaway and it says I need to be returned to my guardian, Mr. Casabian, like I was a runaway child. Unfortunately I also have a second warrant, which really is "unwarranted." I know this is a bad time to joke. The second says that I somehow struck my conservator, Robert Casabian, with my car (untrue) when I was escaping from the creepy group home where he wanted to place me. Also, I have been listed as a missing person by my sister. The detective told me that the Los Angeles court wants me returned. He said that they would have to hold me in custody until I went in front of a judge in Eugene so that he could determine what to do with me. I asked if that meant in jail behind bars and he said I should sit on a bench in the front while he talked to the district attorney to figure out what to do with me but if I decided I wanted to take off I would definitely wind up behind bars. When he also said he was going to call my sister I asked him not to, but he said he had to as she was the one who filed the missing person report. I asked him how they found me and he said that they got a call from an investigation service that Robert Casabian had hired. This makes me especially angry as I am sure my trust had to pay for that investigator just like it pays my lawyer who does nothing but work against me. The police station was pretty quiet as not much happens in Creswell, but I did still have my phone and nothing to do to pass the time and despite my current terror or maybe because of it, I suddenly realized that I could finally upload all 73 Yelp reviews that I had written while I was on the run and kept stored in my phone's SD card memory. It took over an hour with the slow connection to upload them all, but I still had to wait another half hour before Abbie came through the door and found me sitting on the bench. She apologized for taking so long to get here and said that Durinda wanted to come but she asked her not to because Durinda was too upset and right now we need cool heads. Abbie said that she talked to the conservatorship attorney, Harry Chauncy, and he said that I will have to appear in Eugene for a hearing before a judge to determine bail and extradition. He said he would try to expedite it so that I can appear tomorrow but that I would still have to spend the night in custody. I asked if that meant jail and Abbie said that they wanted to send me to the Lane County Jail in Eugene, but that she would talk to the police and see what she could do. I said I really didn't want to spend the night in county jail. She then went to try to find the detective sergeant to talk to him.

Lane County Jail ★ ★

After I was arrested at the Creswell Farmers' market and brought to the Creswell sheriff's station, my friend Abbie Farnham tried everything she could to try to get them to release me back to her farm, promising them that she would make sure I would be at my hearing the next day, but they said that because I was a fugitive that I would have to at least spend the night in the Lane County Jail in Eugene. I have never been in jail and it is one thing to see someone go to jail on TV and another to actually be in one for the first time. When Abbie complained at the sheriff's station that I could have a severe meltdown if they put me in a cell, they did give me a consent form to sign that said I had mental health issues and would need special treatment. I hated to sign that form because I don't really want people to think I have a "mental health issue" which to most people is the same as crazy. The jail is a big place and first they put me in a room where an intake person with a badge reading "Wendy Frankel" came in. She said she was a therapist but when I asked her to tell me what her degrees were she wouldn't tell me. My own Dr. DeSantis has MD and PhD degrees from UCLA and USC. She asked me a series of dumb questions like if I was thinking about killing myself. If I seriously was I probably wouldn't tell her. When I asked for Zoloft because all of mine was at the farm she said I would have to wait to see if the jail doctor could prescribe it and he wouldn't be back until tomorrow. Then a guard took me to my cell. They do have a section for people with "special issues" that has single cells with windows and there is a common area with a television. In my cinderblock cell there was a bed, a little desk, a sink and a metal toilet with no toilet seat where anybody could look in while I am using it. The bed was thin and hard with coarse sheets and light came from a naked dim bulb in the ceiling. I could hear a TV playing loudly outside and voices coming from the common area. It was like being in the world's worst group home. I was so tired I went to sleep anyway. The next morning I got up and went to the common room hoping for something to eat. The television was tuned to KEZI Eugene morning news and after a few moments I was on it! They were showing somebody's cell phone video of when I was being arrested yesterday at the Creswell Farmers' market and how people there tried to stop the police from taking me in, chanting "let him go!" The TV reporter said that I was living at a retreat for autistic people (semi-true) and that I had been arrested for a hit-and-run incident in Los Angeles (also semi-true). Then I saw my pro bono attorney from Americans Against Guardianship Abuse, Harry Chauncy, being interviewed and he told the interviewer about what a miscarriage of justice it was for a court-appointed conservator to be able to take away a person's rights and how I was a competent adult being abused by a system that encourages fraud and theft.

Lane County Circuit Court ★ ★ ★ ★ ★

I came to Lane County Circuit Court today because there was a hearing to see if I would be sent back to the court in California to face charges of felony hit-and-run and running away from my conservator. I was brought to the court on a police transport van from the Lane County Jail where I had been kept against my will the previous night. When I got in the van the driver told me that he had seen me on KVAL news this morning, which is different from KEZI where I saw it, and that means that I must have been seen on at least two stations. When I was escorted by a policewoman into the courtroom, I saw that nearly everyone from High Meadow Farm (where I am a temporary resident) was sitting in the back. Abbie Farnham, who runs the farm, was there, and my friend Durinda waved to me. Then Tiffany held up a cardboard sign to me that said "FREE MARCUS KATZ!!!" and I saw the bailiff go over to her and tell her to put it down. The policewoman led me to a place to stand in front of Judge Theresa Romano and then Harry Chauncy, my pro bono attorney, stood up there next to me. Judge Romano looked at my records on a computer screen in front of her and then asked me if I had ever hit someone in Los Angeles with my car. I said that I was sure that I hadn't. She said that apparently the Los Angeles court thinks differently. Judge Romano asked me how I managed to get all the way to Oregon while there was a warrant out and I told her it took me a while after my car broke down and Mr. Casabian froze my credit card and bank accounts. She said this made her wonder why I needed a guardian if I was capable of traveling almost a thousand miles on my own with no money. Then Harry Chauncy told her that I was in fact the victim of a scheme to siphon off my mother's estate by a dishonest conservator. Judge Romano then asked me if Mr. Chauncy was my attorney of record and Mr. Chauncy interrupted to say that because I was under a conservatorship, under law I was unable to hire an attorney on my own, but that he was appearing as a friend of the court with the judge's permission. It was at that moment that Frank Tuttle, the attorney that the Los Angeles probate court has chosen for me against my will, arrived at court, and introduced himself to Judge Romano, saying he was my court-appointed attorney and he would represent me. He said that I should be returned to Los Angeles where, as my attorney of record, he would defend me against the hit-and-run charges (ha!). Judge Romano seemed surprised to see him and asked if he had flown up all the way from Los Angeles just for this hearing and Frank Tuttle said he came because he was concerned for his client. That is when Harry Chauncy said to the judge that the only reason he came all the way up was so he could bill hours and expenses to my account. Frank Tuttle then wanted to know who Harry Chauncy was because he was the only attorney the Los Angeles court had appointed to represent me. Harry Chauncy asked the judge to check if Frank Tuttle, a California attorney, was "admitted" in an Oregon Court. When Frank Tuttle replied that he wasn't, Judge Romano, who was clearly not liking Frank Tuttle from the start, told him he would have to enlist an Oregon attorney if he wanted to represent me in his court. Frank Tuttle wasn't pleased and said he had contacted an Oregon attorney who canceled at the last minute. Harry Chauncy pointed out to the judge that the California court was actually making me pay for Tuttle's incompetence and that Tuttle had no intention to actually defend me. The judge nodded and said that Mr. Tuttle would have to sit down in the audience if he wanted to stay at all. Then Tiffany yelled out "Yayyyyhh!!" from the back of the room. Judge Romano told her to be quiet or leave. Then Judge

Romano turned to me and asked again if I had hit someone with my car and I said that I didn't think I had and then Harry Chauncy spoke up and said that he had evidence to show that the charge was fraudulent and that I would be hamstrung to defend myself in Los Angeles with an attorney hired by my tormentor, Mr. Casabian. The judge said that she couldn't hear the case herself as it was a California matter but asked him what he had to show regarding the warrant and Harry offered up his laptop computer and said he had surveillance footage that an associate in Los Angeles had obtained from the liquor store across the street. This was a big surprise to me. It was grainy video, but it showed clearly that the supposed victim, Robert Casabian, my conservator, ran after my car as I was driving away from the group home and then banged hard on the trunk of the car from behind as I sped off, probably because he was really mad. Anyone could see from the video that I never could hit him as he came from behind. After the judge saw the video she ruled that she would accept a motion to delay extraditing me to California for the time being while Mr. Chauncy appealed to the California courts. Mr. Chauncy said that an associate lawyer in his organization would be filing suit in Los Angeles shortly asking that Mr. Casabian be removed and separately that the conservatorship be dissolved. The judge said that I would have to put up $200 bail in the meantime which she said is the minimum amount they could ask. Abbie Farnham gave the bailiff a credit card for me and then I was free to leave.

Mezza Luna Pizzeria ★ ★ ★ ★ ★

Mezza Luna is better than none. (FYI "mezza" means "half" in Italian.) After things went very well for me at the Lane County Courthouse, my friends from High Meadow Farm who had come to court to watch me all wanted to hang out and have pizza at Mezza Luna Pizzeria which is only two blocks from the courthouse. I was very anxious to go back to the farm to see my dog, Sadie, whom I hadn't seen in two days, but it was important to see and thank all my supporters who came to my hearing. My pro bono attorney, Harry Chauncy, whose brilliance saved me today, said that he would stop in for just a few minutes as he had to get back to his office, but he warned me that it was really too early to celebrate and that I might win this round, but it is still very hard to break a court-ordered conservatorship. There were nine of us including me so we put three tables together. I hoped Durinda would sit next to me, but she chose to sit at the other end and when I looked at her she didn't look back which made me nervous. We all shared a "stinky garden pizza" (gorgonzola cheese, mushroom spinach and garlic), a "Schmo2 pizza" (chicken sausage and mushrooms) and a "Marge pizza" (simple tomato sauce and mozzarella). They had a thin crust and high quality ingredients with fresh mushrooms, not canned. Maybe a wood-fired oven would have made for a crisper crust, but I don't want to be too picky as the pizza did taste excellent. The manager walked directly over to me and wanted to know if everything was okay and if I liked my pizza. When I said I thought it was really good he said he recognized me from TV and he had already seen all of the 73 newly updated reviews that I posted while I was sitting in the Creswell police station. He said that he noticed I already had around hundreds of new likes and he heard people in the restaurant were talking about me and my case. I guess I'm famous now and this made Harry Chauncy happy because being in the news and getting publicity would definitely help my case. When we finished, Durinda told everyone she had to go to work in her lab in Eugene. I asked if I could walk her to her car. She said I could if I wanted to, but I could tell something was wrong. When we got outside she said she had read all my newly posted reviews last night and she wanted to know if I really thought she had a bad singing voice which I guess I said in my review of bingo night at the Creswell VFW when we sang songs from *The Music Man* in front of the crowd. She said she felt really humiliated by my review. I realized I had made a big mistake and I hurt her feelings. I told her I was sorry, but I try always to be honest when I review. Durinda said she didn't know why it was necessary to talk about her singing at all when the review was about bingo. I was going to say something to defend myself and about how the reviews weren't always about the places I am reviewing, but Durinda said that she really needed to get back to the lab and she got into her car. I wanted to apologize more, but I didn't. I know that being on the spectrum can make me too critical of others, and I wondered whether what I did by talking about her singing was inappropriate. But even though I may be hard on others, Dr. DeSantis has pointed out that I am also often too critical of myself. Am I being too critical of myself now? And is Durinda mad at me because she is being too critical of herself? I really wish I never wrote about Durinda's singing.

Creswell Pharmacy ★★★★★

This is a very good drugstore and most of the people at High Meadow Farm come here. When I needed my refill of Zoloft, the pharmacist was able to call my doctor in Los Angeles and fill the prescription quickly. Also they have a very nice selection of small gifts and cards. That is why I stopped in here today. Despite all that was going good in my life the past few days I was suffering because Durinda was really mad at me for having written critically about how she sings. Because I have pledged to be truthful here I am still not able to say that Durinda is a great singer, but she has many other really fine qualities and I wish I hadn't written what I wrote. She is very smart and an expert in her field of ichthyology. She is a very caring person who has been kind and helpful not only to me, but to everyone at High Meadow Farm where she is really loved and also she is very good at fixing cars and machinery. Those are more fine qualities than most people have and I really don't care if she is a great or a terrible singer. I looked around on the gift aisle and I found what I wanted right away. It was a really cute plush toy chicken whose tag said she was named Pepper the Mottled Hen. At the farm, Durinda has a favorite hen whose name is Chloe and Chloe has mottled black feathers and looks just like Pepper. Chloe doesn't get along with the other hens very well and is a bit of a loner (we joke that she is on the spectrum too) but she does like people and Durinda especially, and will sometimes fly up and sit in her lap. I picked out a blank greeting card with a picture of a farm on the front even though it didn't look very much like High Meadow Farm. Inside I wrote, "My friend Marcus is very sad that you are angry with him and that he upset you and wants you to be his friend, too. Won't you please forgive him?" and I signed it "Chloe the Chicken." I also crossed out "Pepper" and wrote "Chloe" on the tag on the toy chicken and I will give it to her along with the card. I hope Durinda laughs and I hope she forgives me.

Bijou Art Theater ★ ★ ★ ★ ★

My friend Durinda bought tickets for us to see *Hell's Angels*, a classic 1930 movie about World War I pilots with amazing scenes of aerial combat. I apologized to her for writing that she had a bad singing voice. She accepted my apology for criticizing her singing voice and we have been getting along fine since then. She said she was really amazed and impressed when she read in my reviews about all of the exciting adventures I had getting to Oregon. Yesterday she bought us movie tickets because I had once told her that the best movies ever made about airplanes were *Hell's Angels*, *The Right Stuff*, *Wings*, *United 93*, *Sully*, and *Air Force*. *Hell's Angels* doesn't have the best movie story, but it has some of the best dogfight sequences ever filmed. The Bijou Art Theater is in what used to be a church and, believe it or not, the pews have been replaced by movie seats and the screen is where the altar might have been. Wow! I hope God doesn't mind ☺. There are tables in a center garden where you can sit and have coffee and snacks. That was really nice of Durinda to take me here. I don't think she is as interested in airplanes as I am but she did it to make me happy because I have been on quite an emotional roller coaster with all of the legal things that have been happening. Although my AAGA lawyer in Los Angeles did manage to get my hit-and-run charge dismissed and Mr. Chauncy has managed through a series of legal maneuvers to keep me in Oregon, he has been unable so far to undo my conservatorship which means among other things that I have no access to any of the money in my estate and Mr. Casabian continues to spend what he wants from my estate to fight me in court. It is frightening to think that I might have to leave Creswell now that I am so settled at High Meadow Farm where Sylvan recently put me in charge of our small grove of fifteen Rubinette apple trees and I have been learning all about pruning and harvesting. I prune the young trees to make sure the branches all reach out to place the apples into the sunshine. Also I ride in to Eugene with Durinda on Wednesdays and Saturdays to be a docent at the Oregon Air Museum. I especially like Wednesdays when young school children often will come in with their teacher. I think Durinda really liked the movie *Hell's Angels*. At least she said she did and she was really impressed when I identified all of the planes for her in the big dogfight scene which I read they shot in Glendale, California, about fifteen miles from my old house in Santa Monica, although in the movie it is supposed to take place over Germany. Three pilots crashed and died in the making of the movie. I bought the popcorn and the drinks because Durinda bought the tickets. After she drank all of her Coke, she asked if she could sip some of mine. Normally I don't like to share drinks with anyone as I am germaphobic, but I gave her my Coke and then had a sip myself after she did. I guess that is proof that she is somebody special to me.

The Craft Place ★ ★ ★

Yesterday, when my friend Durinda and I went to the movies, we passed by The Craft Place where you can purchase plates and coffee cups that are plain and then paint them. Durinda said she had always been meaning to try it so we went there the next day. We didn't call it a date, but if it wasn't, it was awfully close. They supply the paint and they have books with suggestions about things you might paint and they also have stencils if (like me) you aren't that good at drawing. Durinda insisted she was treating me because it was her idea even though she had paid for the movie yesterday and she bought two coffee cups for us to decorate. Durinda said she was going to paint a zebrafish design on hers and I said I would paint a DC3 airplane on mine. Elise, the woman who worked there, helped us out and explained that first we should do pencil drawings on the cups and then we could paint. We sat together at a table. Durinda can draw really well and she made a really nice design. I pulled up a picture of a DC3 on my phone for a reference. It had Douglas Aircraft factory markings on the side, but there was no way I was going to be able to draw those. I noticed that Durinda was blinking her eyes a lot. I asked her what was wrong and she said that she was having trouble with the fluorescent lights. I have seen this a few times before with her as, like many people on the spectrum, certain frequencies of light that come off of fluorescents will bother them and often give them headaches. Fluorescent lights don't bother me so much, but I am very sensitive to certain harsh sounds so I can relate to her problem. She pulled a cap with a big brim out of her handbag and put that on and tried to finish drawing, but it wasn't working. Then she asked Elise if she could turn off the lights as it was a problem for her. There was plenty of daylight coming in the front window and no other people in the store. Elise acted like this was some weird thing to ask for and said that the owner of the store wanted her to keep the lights on so that people knew the store was open. She wasn't mean about it, but she said that she couldn't turn them off even after Durinda asked a second time. Durinda said she was going to have to leave, but that I could stay and finish my cup, but of course I said I would go too and we left the cups there. I think Elise should have at least offered our money back, but she didn't. When we got outside Durinda said that she should have followed my example and brought up the ADA (Americans with Disabilities Act) the way I did in my very first Yelp review with Barrington Farms Market when they wouldn't turn off the trumpet music that disturbed me on their store speakers. She wished she had been braver and stronger with Elise. I am not sure that would have been a good thing, but I know how she feels. Then she said something very interesting. She said that she didn't know why my conservator wasn't violating the Americans with Disabilities Act when he tried to put me in a group home against my will just because of my disability. I didn't have an answer for that, but I thought it was a good question to ask my pro bono attorney, Harry Chauncy.

Eugene Power House ★ ★ ★

You will be shocked (at the prices)! I think it's cool that this restaurant is a genuine 1920 electric power station and they did a big remodel to make this an upscale and hipstery place to eat. It's not the kind of place I would go to on my own, but my sister, Lisa, flew up to visit me in Creswell. This is the first time I have seen her since running away. She first came to High Meadow Farm and after I gave her a tour of the farm, Abbie Farnham invited her to have lunch with the group at the farm table, but Lisa said that she wanted to have some time alone with me and had to catch a five o'clock plane back. While driving with her in her rented car she said a lawyer in her firm who is from Eugene suggested Eugene Power House. She said that she thought it would be a great opportunity for me to write one of my Yelp reviews and I guess she was right as I can't afford any of the more upscale restaurants in Eugene. Part of me was glad to see my sister although things are strained between us since she tried to become my conservator after my mother died. In the car I told her more about the farm and she told me about my niece and nephew, Elizabeth and Adam. She said they are doing very well and that Elizabeth is a star forward on her soccer team and Adam was accepted for third grade in Curtis School up on Mulholland Drive which, according to Lisa, is very hard to get into and she had to pull every string to find someone on the board of directors to write a letter for him. Adam is very smart and I wouldn't be surprised if he could have gotten in on his own. At the restaurant I ordered the Dungeness crab mac-and-cheese appetizer and prime rib. Lisa got a beet salad and seared scallops. Lisa said that the food was just okay and that food is better in Los Angeles. She is probably right, but I guess I didn't like it that she was trying to make Eugene sound bad. I thought my crab mac cheese was delicious although my prime rib was a little too fatty and overdone. But the food was definitely better than the conversation. Although Lisa said she was coming up just to see me, I know she doesn't show up unless she has a reason. First she said that everything that happened to me was my own fault because I had created a big mess by trying to bring in my stepfather, Carl, as my conservator after she applied for conservatorship "for my benefit." She said that if I had just let her be conservator we could have worked something out about where I would live and I caused so much trouble in court it was my fault that the judge chose an outside conservator. She said that she didn't like Mr. Casabian either and he had actually forbidden her to see me but she came anyway. She said she is unable to even get an accounting of how much of my estate Casabian is spending, but she is certain that he is doing everything he can to take money that I might need and that someday could go to Elizabeth and Adam. She didn't say "when I die" but of course that is what she meant. She said that she had found a good attorney that could petition the court to have Mr. Casabian removed and replaced with her, but she would need my support in court. I would have to testify to how badly Mr. Casabian had treated me and also I would have to tell Carl not to interfere this time. I wanted to know that if she was conservator would I be able to have my apartment back, but she would only say that it would be a "good topic for conversation." I told her that I didn't think I wanted her attorney. She said that it was my best choice as without her I wouldn't have any money or resources to fight Mr. Casabian on my own. I didn't want to tell her too much, but I said that I already have an attorney working for me and he isn't charging for it. Lisa seemed pretty annoyed and said "you get what you pay for" with "do-good lawyers," but I don't necessarily agree with that. Then I said that I needed to get back to the farm and I didn't want to talk about it anymore. That made her really mad and she started talking loud, practically yelling at me, even though we were in a restaurant. She said that Mother really spoiled me because of my autism and trained me to always get my way. I don't think that is true. She said that she had wasted her time coming up and would order an Uber ride for me to go home as she needed to get to the airport. That was okay with me. She paid the bill that I saw was $118.40. Even if I ever get my estate back I don't think I will find myself spending that much just for lunch.

Portland Oregonian Newspaper ★ ★ ★ ★ ★

Many of the Yelp reviews for *The Oregonian* are negative, but the majority of complaints are about subscribers getting their paper delivered wet or late or sometimes people are mad because the paper wrote something positive about a Democrat and a Republican thought that was biased or vice versa. I know *The Oregonian* is the biggest paper in the Northwest and it is much respected. Even though I live in Eugene (Creswell actually), 118 miles away from Portland, *The Oregonian* did a half-page story in their Sunday edition about me and High Meadow Farm and my fight with Robert Casabian and the Los Angeles Probate Court. A week ago, Mary Beth Stevens, a reporter, came down to High Meadow Farm and interviewed me and the farm director, Abbie Farnham, and took pictures of us and the farm. She asked a lot of questions about me and my escape to Oregon and about how I wound up being a fugitive. I know that reporters shouldn't necessarily have personal opinions reporting news, but when she heard my story she said it made her angry and she hoped I would win in court. She said that based on what she knows from her research it is very hard to win cases like mine. The article came out yesterday and it has a picture of me and my dog, Sadie, while I am trimming one of the apple trees on the farm. It talked about my journey to get to Oregon and how the court in California had been so unfair to me. Neither Judge Hughes in the Los Angeles Probate Court or Robert Casabian would allow themselves to be interviewed and I think that just made them look worse. The article also talked about how I have written 374 Yelp reviews and how I now have over 1800 followers on Yelp and that many of them have written on Twitter, Reddit and Facebook that I should be freed from my conservator. My so-called court-appointed attorney, Frank Tuttle, said that he couldn't talk to the press about a court matter (totally untrue), but he said that in general the probate system works very well. (Hah!) BTW I still haven't heard anything about my request for Elite status. Are you listening, Yelp Elite?

Byner, Selvin and Kaplan Law Offices ★ ★ ★ ★ ★

Harry Chauncy, my *pro bono* attorney, asked if Abbie Farnham and I could meet him and a lawyer named Cheryl Kraft at Byner Selvin and Kaplan, a national law firm with an office in Portland. Portland is an hour and a half drive, so I guessed that this had to be important. The offices were in a high rise building and we met Cheryl Kraft in a conference room with a big table and lots of chairs and you could see the Willamette River out of the big windows. It was way fancier than Harry Chauncy's office which is small and really kind of a mess. Cheryl Kraft's assistant asked if we would like water or coffee and I asked for water and she asked me if I wanted sparkling and I said yes and she brought real Pellegrino. After all the introductions, Ms. Kraft said that Harry Chauncy had reached out to her to help with my case and that she found it very interesting. Mr. Chauncy said he looked into my suggestion (really my friend Durinda's) to file a lawsuit under the Americans with Disabilities Act which he thought was an interesting idea. He said the theory would be that by assigning me a conservator and stuffing me into a group home they were taking away the rights of a disabled person which is prohibited by law under the Americans with Disabilities Act. (Even though I don't think I am really a disabled person, sometimes it can be handy to be considered one.) When he researched it he found that an attorney in the Las Vegas office of the large firm of Byner, Selvin and Kaplan had already filed exactly that kind of law suit for another client and that it was working its way through the court there. He also learned that Cheryl Kraft, who is based in their Los Angeles office, had done work on that law suit and happened to be visiting their Portland office right now, so he set up this meeting. Then Cheryl spoke. She said that she had already read all about me and I was getting pretty famous. I said I was trying not to get a swelled head and she laughed. She said she was excited to meet me in person and that I was a good candidate to try the same strategy in California if I would be willing. She said that her firm does a lot of *pro bono* work and her bosses okayed it for her to join with Mr. Chauncy if that was alright with me (duhh... yes!). They would file a suit against Robert Casabian for violating the ADA as well as my fourteenth amendment rights which say that no one can take away my liberty without due process of law. Then they would seek to dissolve the conservatorship in Los Angeles court. I asked if this worked if I could then get "supported decision making" (SDM) like my friend Ronan at the farm has. That means that I can choose a team of advisors to help me with important decisions about life and money, but I would still be legally on my own. I think SDM would be great for me as I am not perfect in making all decisions, but I think I am good at recognizing smart, good people and respecting their advice. If I had SDM I would choose Abbie Farnham, Emma Reese at Northwestern Trust and my stepfather, Carl, to be on my team. Mr. Chauncy said we could certainly try for that and Ms. Kraft said none of this could happen overnight, but I have given Byner, Selvin and Kaplan five stars because I would so much like to believe this will all work out and also because they gave me free 16 oz. Pellegrino water ☺.

Dr. Hamza Abassi, DVM ★ ★ ★ ★ ★

Yesterday I was helping Tiffany feed the chickens when all of a sudden the dogs started barking like crazy about something out by the back fence. Sometimes Loki or Shadow will take off after a rabbit or a squirrel and Sadie will run with them just to be one of the gang, but this didn't sound like that. Then I heard yelping and crying and I knew right away it was Sadie. I ran back there as fast as I could and I saw that Loki and Shadow were barking all excited and my friend Sylvan was already there yelling at a big old coyote who had jumped the fence and was escaping into the field. Then I saw Sadie on the ground crying and trying to nurse her hind quarter. There was a big, awful bleeding wound where she had been attacked and you could see her muscle under the fur. It was awful! Sylvan said that Loki, who is part pit bull, went after the coyote and defended Sadie. Tiffany came out of the main house with a dish rag and pressed it on Sadie who was still bleeding. Then Sylvan helped me get Sadie into the van and I held her as he drove as fast as he could to Dr. Abassi's clinic in Creswell. Sadie was shivering and crying the whole way and I thought I might cry myself, but I knew Sadie was depending on me and I held her tight and pressed the towel on the wound. When we got to the clinic I ran in the front door where Rachel, Dr. Abbasi's assistant, took her out of my arms. Dr. Abassi immediately came out from where he was with another animal and they put Sadie on the examining table. He said she was in shock and had to have fluids right away. He put a catheter in her and Rachel put a space blanket around her to keep her warm and I hugged her and I tried so hard to stay strong because she was looking at me like I was the only one who could save her. After about fifteen minutes she stopped crying and was seeming better and Dr. Abbasi cleaned the wound and sewed her up. He said they would have to keep her overnight, which I know was the right thing to do, although I would worry about her the whole time. I asked if I could just stay there overnight, but of course they said that wouldn't work and I understood. Dr. Abbasi saved Sadie and I am really, really grateful. Thanks Dr. Abbasi.

Creswell Dairy Queen ★ ★ ★ ★ ★

This DQ is OK! My friend Durinda insisted on driving me to pick up my dog, Sadie, from the vet today, even though she had to call in to say she wouldn't be going to work. Sadie had been mauled by a coyote and Dr. Abassi, the vet, had kept her overnight. We stopped at the Creswell Dairy Queen because we were too early to pick up Sadie as it was 10:45 and the vet told me she would be ready at 11 a.m. Durinda said she would like some coffee so we went to the drive-up window. I don't drink coffee, but Durinda says she likes their coffee and she orders it with sugar and double cream. I do like Dairy Queen Blizzards though, and I ordered a Choco Brownie Extreme. I think Blizzards are every bit as good as the McFlurries at McDonalds and they come in more flavors and more sizes. Creswell Dairy

Queen keeps their store very clean and also the people who work there are friendly.

I couldn't wait to see Sadie. Last night I was really upset and worried about her and Durinda brought me a dinner plate from the main house. Later, Durinda was telling me about some new computer program she was using at work, I think mostly to calm me down, but I might not have been listening and I kind of curled up on my bed because I just wanted to be quiet. We didn't talk for a little while and then she asked me if it would make me feel better if she cuddled me a bit. Wow!! Part of me was thinking I wish I had a sick dog years ago. (Sorry Sadie. Just kidding.) I said yes to Durinda and she crawled into the bed next to me and put her front up against my back and we lay there a while and I think you would call that spoons. Durinda felt kind of soft and warm and I was thinking that is much better than a hard, skinny girl. She told me that Sadie would be fine and she would drive me to pick her up in the morning and she said I was a very caring person and that's why I was so upset. It's weird that I fell asleep, but I think it was because I was just so stressed. I think dogs sometimes do that. Durinda wasn't there when I woke up. I know that Durinda has feelings for me and I think that is definitely working both ways.

Harry Holt Memorial Park ★ ★ ★ ★

Not just a walk in the park! I don't know who Harry Holt was, but I am glad that there is this park in Creswell that was named after him. It is a small neighborhood park and not very fancy but it has a playground and a covered picnic area. Now that my dog, Sadie, has pretty much healed from being bitten by a coyote (although we are still waiting for all of her fur to grow back where the vet had to shave it), I sometimes take her here to do her business. Occasionally I will bring a snack and eat it in on a bench in the picnic area and just watch the people for a while. Once I sat on a swing and a woman came up and told me that the swings are only for the children. There weren't any children around or I wouldn't have been using it. Although people in Creswell are almost all very friendly and know most of the residents at High Meadow Farm, I think that maybe this woman was different and maybe she thought I was suspicious. Anyway I got off the swing and said I was sorry, even though I wasn't. I don't think that incident should affect my rating of the park, but they could be better about emptying the trash cans so I am giving it four stars.

Now the big news!!! I was walking Sadie in Harry Holt Park when my phone rang. It was my attorney, Harry Chauncy. He said he was calling to tell me some really good news. My conservator, Robert Casabian, was forced to plead *nolo contendere* (really the same as guilty) to statute 148.5 of the California Penal Code which is for filing a false police report. Mr. Chauncy said this is a misdemeanor and unfortunately he won't go to jail but the judge fined him $1000 and Mr. Chauncy says Judge Hughes will have no choice but to remove him as my conservator and I can even sue Robert Casabian for damages. Mr. Chauncy said that we could settle at the very least for the amount of money he wrongly took from my trust fund. What I really want most is to be able to choose where I live and with whom and Mr. Chauncy said that today was a giant step in that direction. I was so excited I wanted to tell Durinda right away and I called her at work even though I know she doesn't like to use work time for personal calls. I told her everything that Harry Chauncy told me, but she still wanted to know more, like how soon I could petition to end the conservatorship. She was almost as excited as I was and she told me how happy she was for me. Then, without even thinking about it, instead of saying goodbye, I said "I love you" to her. I just kind of blurted it out, but I know it came from a place way inside me. I think maybe she was surprised, because she didn't answer right away, but then she said "I love you, too." What a day!

The Peaceable Palate Food Truck ★ ★ ★ ★ ★

It's a party! Abbie Farnham had decided that we needed to have a big party to celebrate what she called my "emancipation." It has been a year since I first came to High Meadow Farm and a lot has happened, most of it good. Really good. The Peaceable Palate food truck parks at the south end of the Creswell Farmers' market on Tuesday. It is owned by Merlin and Nicole who serve locally sourced organic food. They buy some of their vegetables from High Meadow Farm where I work and they have become friends of mine. They stood up for me when the sheriff came to arrest me at the farmers' market two months ago. Today they parked on the gravel by the edge of the garden and served rice bowls, wraps and smoothies. Also they served my favorite thing on their menu, a mushroom avocado quesadilla. There were seventy-four guests as well as two news crews. Abbie had tents and tables set up just for the occasion. I don't think I am really that comfortable with so much attention, but Abbie said it was important to be an inspiration to other people who get stuck in court conservatorships.

After I had been on the news not only in Eugene, but in Los Angeles and even on CNN (they showed the old surveillance video of Robert Casabian banging on the trunk of my car as I escaped), I won my war of independence from my conservators. Also it was a long and difficult battle in court, and I have already spent too much time talking about legal matters but I was so lucky to have found people to take up my cause and last month my conservatorship was officially dissolved in Los Angeles Court. Abbie helped me with my guest list for the party, which may not exactly fall under her official duties as one of my official SDM (Supported Decision Making) team, along with Carl, my stepfather, Dr. DeSantis, and Emma Reese at Northern Trust Bank. Knowing I have their support has given me confidence to make decisions for myself and it is so much better than having a conservator who just tells me what to do. Everyone from the farm came, plus Harry Chauncy and Cheryl Kraft. I invited Francisco, the rodeo cowboy, who took me from Lone Pine to Reno. He couldn't make it but sent me congratulations and also he sent me a first place calf roping ribbon from the 2014 Muscogee Nation Rodeo as an engagement present. Roger, the pilot who flew me from Reno to Eugene came. And so did Carl, who was back from his tour with Bobby Allen and planning next to sail to Tahiti on his boat. I was really happy to see him again. Sadie recognized him and licked his hand!

When I decided I wanted to ask Durinda to marry me I was glad I didn't have to ask permission from a conservator who would probably turn me down as they nearly all do to other people like me in their charge. Instead I just asked Carl and Abbie for their advice and I am so happy to say that they both thought it was a very good idea, although they were concerned that I might be disappointed if Durinda said no. I was concerned, too! But Durinda said yes! Both Abbie and Dr. DeSantis thought it would be smart to wait a bit and let the excitement die down and also let everything sink in. Durinda and I agreed and if all goes well we will get married next summer. Abbie said that we can live in the straw bale house that the farm is building, although it is taking longer than we thought. Now that I have become so famous, I hope you don't mind, but I have decided to be more modest and not so public about all of the details of my life. Being famous isn't 100% wonderful (maybe just 80%) and Abbie had to put up a gate on the driveway to the farm because so many people came to find me and High Meadow. I don't want to talk about sex at all, except to say I am no longer a twenty-two-year-old virgin. Subject closed. And one last thing. Before dessert (cheesecake made by Alison's Republic of Cheesecakes who have a farmers' market food stand) Durinda stood up in front of the whole crowd and told everyone she had a special surprise for me. She smiled like she was going to burst. Then a woman wearing a black business suit walked in and introduced herself to everyone as Jane Stotmeyer. She said she was the executive marketing manager of Yelp in San Francisco. OMG!!! She had a special announcement to make. She asked me to come stand up next to her and I did. Everyone was very quiet while she spoke up so everybody could hear. She said that she and the rest of her team had followed my story with great interest on Yelp. She said she had been in contact with the Yelp Elite executive committee and with the Oregon chapter of Yelp Elites and that it was now her great pleasure to welcome me as an official new member of Yelp Elite. Not only that, but she had a gold badge, normally reserved for Elite members after five years, but specially awarded to me because of my extraordinary story and then she pinned it on my shirt. Everybody there was taking pictures and applauding. I am now Marcus Katz, Yelp Elite! Deal with it!

The End

Acknowledgments

There is a large community that advocates for those who have been unjustly ensnared in rapacious conservatorships, particularly for those on the autism spectrum, and I admire them and greatly appreciate their help. Thanks to Linda Kincaid of the Coalition for Elder and Disability Rights (CEDAR) and Dr. Sam Sugar of Americans Against Abusive Probate Guardianship. I would particularly like to thank Orrin Onken, a lawyer and talented author, for his help with the legal aspects of the story. Also I appreciate the help of Greg Demer and the volunteers at the Santa Monica Museum of Flying. Thanks to Shelley Wiseman for her warm encouragement and sound editorial advice.

"Free Marcus Katz" is a work of fiction. Names places and incidents are either products of the author's imagination or are used fictitiously. This author is a Yelp fan and an ardent online reader and poster, but neither Yelp nor the Yelp community is associated with this work and Yelp has not authorized this book. The author has taken some liberties with the Yelp format, but hopes that the democratic spirit of the Yelp platform shines through. The author is not an attorney and one would be well advised to consult a bona fide lawyer for legal advice regarding conservatorship law and not rely on anything written here. That said, it is hoped that this work inspires examination of the injustices often served to some on the autism spectrum and to those affected by reckless forced conservatorships.

ROUNDFIRE
BOOKS

FICTION

Put simply, we publish great stories. Whether it's literary or
popular, a gentle tale or a pulsating thriller, the connecting theme
in all Roundfire fiction titles is that once you pick them up you
won't want to put them down.
If you have enjoyed this book, why not tell other readers by
posting a review on your preferred book site.

Recent bestsellers from Roundfire are:

The Bookseller's Sonnets
Andi Rosenthal

The Bookseller's Sonnets intertwines three love stories with a tale of religious identity and mystery spanning five hundred years and three countries.

Paperback: 978-1-84694-342-3 ebook: 978-184694-626-4

Birds of the Nile
An Egyptian Adventure
N.E. David

Ex-diplomat Michael Blake wanted a quiet birding trip up the Nile – he wasn't expecting a revolution.

Paperback: 978-1-78279-158-4 ebook: 978-1-78279-157-7

Blood Profit$
The Lithium Conspiracy
J. Victor Tomaszek, James N. Patrick, Sr.

The blood of the many for the profits of the few... *Blood Profit$* will take you into the cigar-smoke-filled room where American policy and laws are really made.

Paperback: 978-1-78279-483-7 ebook: 978-1-78279-277-2

The Burden
A Family Saga
N.E. David

Frank will do anything to keep his mother and father apart. But he's carrying baggage – and it might just weigh him down ...

Paperback: 978-1-78279-936-8 ebook: 978-1-78279-937-5

The Cause
Roderick Vincent

The second American Revolution will be a fire lit from an internal spark.

Paperback: 978-1-78279-763-0 ebook: 978-1-78279-762-3

Don't Drink and Fly
The Story of Bernice O'Hanlon: Part One

Cathie Devitt

Bernice is a witch living in Glasgow. She loses her way in her life and wanders off the beaten track looking for the garden of enlightenment.

Paperback: 978-1-78279-016-7 ebook: 978-1-78279-015-0

Gag
Melissa Unger

One rainy afternoon in a Brooklyn diner, Peter Howland punctures an egg with his fork. Repulsed, Peter pushes the plate away and never eats again.

Paperback: 978-1-78279-564-3 ebook: 978-1-78279-563-6

The Master Yeshua
The Undiscovered Gospel of Joseph

Joyce Luck

Jesus is not who you think he is. The year is 75 CE. Joseph ben Jude is frail and ailing, but he has a prophecy to fulfil ...

Paperback: 978-1-78279-974-0 ebook: 978-1-78279-975-7

On the Far Side, There's a Boy
Paula Coston
Martine Haslett, a thirty-something 1980s woman, plays hard on the fringes of the London drag club scene until one night which prompts her to sign up to a charity. She writes to a young Sri Lankan boy, with consequences far and long.
Paperback: 978-1-78279-574-2 ebook: 978-1-78279-573-5

Tuareg
Alberto Vazquez-Figueroa
With over 5 million copies sold worldwide, *Tuareg* is a classic adventure story from best-selling author Alberto Vazquez-Figueroa, about honour, revenge and a clash of cultures.
Paperback: 978-1-84694-192-4

Readers of ebooks can buy or view any of these bestsellers by clicking on the live link in the title. Most titles are published in paperback and as an ebook. Paperbacks are available in traditional bookshops. Both print and ebook formats are available online.

Find more titles and sign up to our readers' newsletter at
http://www.johnhuntpublishing.com/fiction

Follow us on Facebook at https://www.facebook.com/JHPfiction
and Twitter at https://twitter.com/JHPFiction